"You young whore, Maggie! You've been making love to yourself!"

"What if I have?" She shook her blond fringe with a hardened impudence.

"Would you like to be made to do it in front of the men who admired you while you were setting out the harness?"

"Don't mind."

I'm sure she did mind, but Mag was too brazen to admit it. I turned her 'round a moment and was not the least surprised by the fading traces of stripes and one or two small bruises on Maggie's bottom-cheeks. It was clear that, when I left after her punishment the other night, one of the grooms had taken Maggie into another room and caned her viciously.

"Very well, Maggie," I said quietly, "the next time you're caught at it, I'll have you strapped for the pony-lash on your bare bottom. How do you like the prospect of that?"

BEAUTY IN THE BIRCH

ANONYMOUS

BLUE MOON BOOKS
NEW YORK

Published by
Blue Moon Books
An Imprint of Avalon Publishing Group Incorporated
161 William St., 16th Floor
New York, NY 10038

ISBN 1-56201-285-1

9 8 7 6 5 4 3 2 1

Printed in the United States of America
Distributed by Publishers Group West

INTRODUCTION

   Birch in the Boudoir was first published in
Paris in 1905, according to its title page, by Charles
Carrington, at 13 Faubourg Montmartre. It was described as "an exchange of intimate letters between a
young lady and a gentleman, recording their true
amatory and disciplinary experiences of an Arabian
harem and an English girls' reformatory establish-
ment." It appeared at the same time in Carrington's
long career of publishing erotica as *Woman and Her
Master*, *The Beautiful Flagellants of New York*, and
Sadopaideia.
   Like *Woman and Her Master* (The story of English girls in Arabian harems after their capture at
Khartoum), *Birch in the Boudoir* was written by
Jean de Villiot. It was a continuation of, or at least a
companion to, the story variously issued as *Venus in
Tight Trousers* and *The Amorous Memoirs of
Capt. Charles De Vane*.
   Who was Jean de Villiot? He was at least two peo-
ple. The main source of Carrington's erotic–
flagellation novels was Hugues Rebell (1868-1905),

poet, essayist, and friend of Oscar Wilde. Rebell would write the first versions of the novels in his own language and Carrington would sometimes publish them as *En Virginie* (for *Dolly Morton*), *La Chambre Jaune* (for *The Yellow Room*), *Venus Fessée* (for *Venus in Tight Trousers*), and La *Conférence expérimentale par le Colonel Cinglant* (for *Colonel Spanker's Experimental Lecture*.)

Rebell was also the author of *Etudes sur la Flagellation*, a work of nonfiction whose later editions included at least such English reformatory scandals as the caning of Elaine Cox, Sally Fenton, Jane Mitchener, and other fourteen-year-olds, by the notorious James Miles. For good measure, there was the incident in which the bare bottom of Sarita, a tall, willowy beauty of fair skin and dark hair, was sadistically caned by the avenging Turks. It was also a Turkish military tribunal, said Rebell, which ordered the apprehension of a fair-skinned, soft-figured, and close-cropped blonde, Janina. The Tribunal watched while nineteen-year-old Janina was strapped bottom-upwards over a cartwheel in front of them and whipped.

Such was the raw material of Rebell's erotic fiction. It was then taken by a second author and turned into colloquial English for export trade! Not surprisingly, it is Rebell's French version which is restrained (the police never confiscated his editions) and the English which is more highly spiced (the police seized these copies by the shelf-load).

Who was the man responsible for turning Rebell's French into racy English—the other half of Jean de Villiot? There are stories of Charles Carrington's hired writers sitting at tall counting-house desks, dashing off flagellation erotica by the yard. The more likely truth is that Carrington, an author in his own right, took the imaginative work of Rebell and touched it up here and there for the English version.

Birch in the Boudoir is a randy story of the kind in which Carrington specialised. But Rebell—whose name might almost be a pun on Rebel—had a radical and subversive streak as a writer. He presents Charlie and Lissie as a pair of young libertines whom society might condemn—but for the much greater corruption of that society itself! In *Birch in the Boudoir,* the police are dishonest to a man: when the venerable old lawyer, Raven, falls out of a toilet-stall with his trousers down and town guardsmen embracing him, the two police officers present would not for the world arrest him; they depart a few minutes later, saluting the old lawyer smartly, their pockets chinking with sovereigns.

When Charlie forcibly uses and whips Noreen, the matter is reported to the local police. Their reaction is to apologise to him for any inconvenience caused. The local constabulary and the magistrates are duly bribed to see that Charlie goes free and Noreen is sternly dealt with. The only problem is that Charlie and his cronies cannot bribe the Lord Chancellor, head of England's legal system. The Lord Chancellor is not incorruptible, being only a politician, as Charlie says, but his price is too high.

Carrington had fled the English law and, like Sade, Rebell is morally rather than sexually outrageous here. The libertines in the story are sympathetic, the moralists and builders of empire are the true ogres. He condemns the latter while never raising an eyebrow over the Pasha Ibrahim, who harnesses a bare-hipped girl between the shafts of his little garden carriage. In a preposterous entrance to the story, Ibrahim appears before the crowd of onlookers: like a courteous sportsman, he bows his acknowledgement of their polite applause, then clambers into the seat, whip in hand.

The learned Dr. Jacobus carries out an experimental lecture upon the sexual features of Lesley, a promiscuous young wife. This is a continuation, or encore, to *Colonel Spanker's Experimental Lecture*. The book, one of Carrington's most popular, had appeared in French and English several years earlier. Before the invited "scholars," Lesley submits to copulation, sodomy, and chastisement. The Schoolmaster, responsible for the last two of these, staggers with exhaustion. There is immediate concern for him, two assistants supporting him from the platform to the sympathetic murmuring of the audience. The plight of the young woman, who has been squirming under his attention, is not a subject for concern.

There is a dark humour in all this. The libertines are the young man and woman who write the letters, also the editor, who joins them in a Postscript. Who are the moralists? Dr. Jacobus is the man of moral science, dedicated to the study of anatomy as the means of punishing female misconduct. He is briefly glimpsed giving Noreen a forced enema, for example. He talks of making Lesley less arrogant and promiscuous by the harem custom of trimming away the sexually sensitive appendages between her legs. He is certainly no libertine: he forces her body's natural functions under discipline. To achieve this, it seems, is the greatest moral reward he can imagine.

The second moralist is the young English Milord, whose life is dedicated to chastising or humiliating sexually any girl with an Asian or Caribbean appearance. His antics with Connie or Jolly recommend him strongly to the men of empire, who see in him a worthy son of those first pioneers, the men who forced their rule upon wayward young women in India or China.

Lastly there is the Schoolmaster, a man whose life is devoted to moral instruction. How the world applauds him, it seems. He is prepared to toil without reward in punishing an adulterous young wife like Lesley, a forward slut like Jackie or Noreen. It may seem a little odd that this also involves copulating with them. Yet, as he explains patiently to Lesley, she has deserted her husband's penis and so now she must be punished by his.

Like Sade himself, Rebell is surely commenting on reality. The young English Milord, the empire builder, had his counterparts in reality. In Jamaica, during the troubles of the 1860s, as Sir William Hardman noted, rebellious young island women were whipped on their bare bottoms by eager young officers—sometimes with piano wire. The only fate suffered by these young sadists was to be welcomed home as heroes and promoted!

The Schoolmaster might surely be a portrait of James Miles and his kind, with whom Rebell was certainly familiar. When Miles was hauled before Rochester magistrates for having inflicted up to forty or fifty birch strokes upon girls like Jennifer Parry or Sarah Barnes, the presiding justices rolled about in Pickwickian laughter at the absurdity of the prosecution. They sent him back to continue his good work. Indeed, a bonus of two shillings and sixpence (about ten dollars) was added for every bare adolescent female bottom he cared to thrash. There were, of course, no compromising pregnancies, but, in his account of the case, Rebell voiced the suspicion that the estimable Mr. Miles was indulging in wholesale sodomy and fellatio with his girls.

In reality, corruption by the moralists may have

6

gone deeper still. The justices who acquitted James Miles had a private interest in the case: they were entitled to sit in the whitewashed punishment room of the reformatory and watch the show. For a whole evening, a procession of adolescent girls knelt over the block with their panties down to be birched or caned. It was a bizarre occasion, a mixture of strip-tease, moral self-righteousness, and sex as a blood-sport like fox-hunting or pigeon-shooting. To have given a verdict against James Miles would have ended these evenings of judicial excitement.

In any case, the justices would have been over-ruled had they condemned him. At the hearing, it was revealed that the youngest female bottom upon which he exercised his talents was ten years old, the oldest twenty-eight! Yet, in 1904, the year of the *Birch in the Boudoir* letters, there appeared Sir James Stephen's *Digest of the Criminal Law* (Sixth Edition). On page eight a clear ruling was laid down: in the punishment of whipping, as the book called it, "the number of strokes and the instrument used are left to the discretion of the person by whom the whipping is inflicted."

Like the moralists of Rebell's fiction, James Miles was entirely within his rights. The state paid him handsomely for indulging his enthusiasms in a man-ner which would cost him a fortune in a brothel. And the public applauded such things. "First-rate disciplinarian," approved Archibald Sinclair in his 1857 *Reminiscences.* "Never gives less than three dozen." The only whiff of illegality is a suggestion that he deliberately rather than accidentally entered the ages of fourteen-year-olds like Elaine Cox, Sally Fenton, or Jane Mitchener, as *sixteen.* By the partic-ular rules of the reformatory, the pony-lash or whipcord could not be used under sixteen, and perhaps the industrious Mr. Miles grew impatient.

The most unlikely moralist in the novel is the maniacal Dr. Jacobus. His punishment enemas and the pruning of a girl between the legs is surely a mad fantasy. Alas, Jacobus might almost have been modelled upon two real-life physicians of the day: Dr. W. Tyler Smith, in the *London Medical Journal* for 1848 (Vol. I, p. 607), proved Dr. Jacobus to be a mere beginner in the so-called punishment enema. Smith's contribution to medical science was to chill the infusion by using ice water. Thus, presumably, the recipient found her lust literally cooled. And Jacos's other unsavoury mania, that of rendering docile any forward or promiscuous young woman by trimming away her clitoris and labia, was once regarded as exclusively a harem custom to stop slave girls spoiling themselves for their masters by secret masturbation. But among Victorian healers of the sick, however, it was also pioneered by Dr. Isaac Baker Brown, whose career made headlines in the *British Medical Journal* for 1867. Defiant or forward adolescent girls were duly trimmed to prevent masturbation. Frisky young women of eighteen or twenty underwent the same fate. Interestingly, his strongest penchant was for pruning promiscuous young wives and thus rendering them more loyal and submissive to their husband's penis. The preoccupation with sexual punishment of the adulterous young wife is parallelled by Jacobus in his vindictive use of Lesley.

The lunacies of Dr. Jacobus are thus the lunacies of society. In the novel, the editor takes up this theme in a sardonic Postscript to his letters. With all these girls at his disposal, what is Jacobus's idea of supreme triumph? It is to see Lesley or Noreen perform the most menial function of their rumps, as he puts it, preferably under punishment. To be offered this aesthetic spectacle is the appropriate reward for the imperialist, the pedagogue, and the man of moral science. Even *The 120 Days of Sodom* would scarcely contradict this subversive political irony.

—RICHARD MANTON

A WORD TO THE READER

      You will readily believe that the letters you are about to read were never intended for publication. They were lately exchanged between a handsome, lusty young gentleman of some thirty summers and a mischievously pretty beauty who had just completed her nineteenth year. As the letters themselves will show, both these friends are persons of the finest breeding and the most amiable liveliness of mind.

I have known handsome Charlie and pretty Lizzie for long enough to assure you that the events which this correspondence relates are utterly worthy of belief. After several months of my urging them, they have at last placed these papers in my hands with full permission to communicate them to the world. They make one stipulation, with which any sensible man or woman must concur: the full names and titles of my young friends are not revealed.

Do you deplore their reticence? Let me tell you then that both Charles and Lizzie are persons of some consequence. So, alas, the most fearful scandal might result from a too impetuous revelation of their identities. Let me say only that the father of our hero is entered in *Burke's Peerage*, while our heroine was presented at court in the second summer of the new King's reign. If you have the curiosity and diligence, you may thus infer their names from the peerage, the court circular, and the details of the letters themselves.

I will not detain you a moment longer than need be from the amorous frolics and ingenious orgies which these two friends witnessed. Yet I must say a word as to how these remarkable letters came into being.

My friend Charlie, a scapegrace lad from youth, is unacknowledged by his noble father and so lives by his wits. As the first letter relates, he was reduced to seek employment at a country mansion where wayward girls were taught the arts of the sewing room and the discipline of the stable. By the example of Miss Martinet, he first observed the amorous effects of chastisement upon a frisky young lady.

What of our beautiful Lizzie? She had accompanied her father, who was Britannia's plenipotentiary in an Arabian territory. A noble Pasha, of European education, made her chivalrously welcome. As the Ambassador's daughter, she was safe from all harm, yet as a woman she was permitted to assist at the pleasures and punishments of the harem. Imagine her surprise and delight on finding that the seraglio was well stocked with English girls as well as with those of warmer colours!

Charlie and Lizzie enjoyed the close mutual attachment which might exist between brother and sister. As a penniless adventurer, it was vain for him to hope that her family would accept him as her suitor. So, when they parted from one another, they agreed to exchange letters, detailing all those amusing incidents of a sexual and disciplinary nature which came their way. The close link of chastisement and erotic excitement was a topic they had discussed often and with great fascination.

You may imagine how interesting their correspondence proved to be! Yet I have no wish to mislead the world. I strongly advise that these letters should not be read by the prudish or the narrow-minded. They will be shocked by the mere sight of a girl opening her legs for a succession of lovers; what will they say when a pretty pupil takes her master's passion in her mouth? Could they endure the sight of a young wife taking her lover's tool surreptitiously in her bottom? They will approve, perhaps, of the whipping of Tania and Vanessa. Yet with what horror will they then see the two naked girls make love together, lying head to tail, using fingers and tongues!

With that word of warning, I will detain you no longer. Charlie and Lizzie shall speak to you now, telling their stories with the lively enthusiasm of youth.

Greystones, 23 April 1904

My dearest Lizzie,

*O*F COURSE you'll say I've been neglecting you, my sweet. Or will you think me downright lazy? "Where is the letter he promised?" you wonder, and a frown wrinkles that beautiful brow of yours!

But that is nothing compared to the astonishment with which you will read the address from which I write. Greystones! What can your very own Charles be doing as assistant in a reformatory for wayward young women? For, alas, I am only the assistant here. It is "Miss Martinet," as the girls call her, who rules the establishment.

Let me explain, my love. On that dreary day of our separation, when your family escorted you from our last rendezvous at the Grosvenor Hotel to the boat-train at Victoria, I was at my wits' end. Bereft of you, and well-nigh penniless, I went back to my rooms in Jermyn Street, paid off the cabbie, and mounted the stairs. I mixed a hock and seltzer, lit a cheroot, and pondered on the beastliness of life. So lost in gloom was I that I did not for a time notice

12

the envelope which the porter had laid upon the table. It bore the imprint of the family lawyers, Raven and Raven, of Gray's Inn Walk.

My first reaction, you may imagine, was to think that it must be a communication from the father who, far from acknowledging me, never had the courtesy to marry my mother. What the deuce, I thought, can the old skinflint want of me now? Ain't he cut me off without a sou already? And ain't that the worst a cove can do to his own flesh and blood?

Had the day been colder and the fire lit, I should have tossed the envelope into its flames. Yet, as it lay there, nothing was to be lost by looking over the contents.

What do you think, Lizzie? It was from old Silas Raven himself, in his crabbed lawyer's script! He presented his compliments to me—the first time the old devil had ever done so—and begged my attendance at his chambers at my earliest convenience. There, he promised, I should learn something to my advantage.

Now, my sweet, all that tosh is a lawyer's way of telling a fellow that there's a pocketful of sovereigns waiting if only he'll have the goodness to fetch 'em. I was down the stairs quicker than old Gladstone's hand up a whore's skirt, for I had scarcely known where my next meal was coming from. I hailed a hansom cab, clambered aboard, and off we went to Gray's Inn Walk, with harness a-jingle and hooves clopping.

If you never meet Silas Raven you won't miss much—he's a spiteful old devil of the prosecuting kind. A ghastly grimacing *phiz,* like a dose of rigor mortis. To my amazement, though, he had set out a tray of glasses and a bottle of fine old Madeira on his desk before my arrival. Hallo, says I to myself, here's a rum go and no mistake!

As the old loon went drivelling on, it appeared he was talking about my Uncle Brandon, an eccentric old bird, who was my Guv'nor's brother. I knew little enough of Uncle Brandon, whose life was vaguely described as "rackety" and who had spent much of it in foreign parts.

When Silas Raven, our cadaverous old brief, informed me that my revered uncle had gone to a better place and left me possessed of his entire estate, I could scarcely believe my ears. That Uncle Brandon's drinking and whoring had made him ripe for plucking I never doubted. Yet I had no idea he had even heard my name, let alone make me his sole heir.

My first impulse was to milk old Silas Raven for a few hundred sovereigns on the spot. Yet it was not to be. The close-fisted senior partner of Raven and Raven read my thoughts. He favoured me with a grin that would have looked unbecoming even on a stoat.

"There is—ahem!—there is a condition attending the legacy of your late uncle. Should you fail to fulfill it, the entire inheritance is to be forfeited and the moneys applied to the Shoreditch Refuge for Penitent Magdalens."

Did you ever read in story books, Lizzie, how a fellow's blood is said to run cold? I never knew the meaning of it till that moment. What need had Penitent Magdalens of the money compared to my own? The senile old curmudgeon grinned at me like a skull.

"You will become possessed of the funds held in trust when you have spent six months in gainful employment, precisely according to your late uncle's instructions. Should you fail. . . ."

Gainful employment? I was not even sure, just then, quite what the term meant. A chap who bets a sov or two on the nags, or lays a wager at baccarat, may gain. Then again, he may lose. I need not have worried, however. My Uncle Brandon had left me no choice.

"Gainful employment!" sneered old Silas Raven. "On Monday next you will take up your post as Assistant Director of Greystones Female Reformatory on the Sussex coast. You will remain thus occupied until further instructions, confided to me by your uncle, are given you."

"Look here!" said I crossly, "suppose they won't have me at this place, wherever it is? Dammit, it ain't justice to bilk a fellow of his inheritance when he can't do what's ordered."

"Have no fear," answered the old swine softly, "your uncle was a benefactor of the Greystones charity. Arrangements are already made for you."

"The devil they are!" said I, quite taken aback.

"Very uncongenial to a shiftless young man of your habits, no doubt!" he murmured, "yet make no mistake, sir! Fail to fulfill the condition and I will see you cut from your uncle's will!"

He would too, I never doubted that! So I left his chambers, descended the steep wooden stairs of the old building, and turned away under the broad trees of Gray's Inn Walk, which were just then coming into early leaf.

All the way back to Jermyn Street in the cab I tried to puzzle out why a randy old uncle I had never seen should leave me all his spondoolicks, and on such conditions. What could it possibly matter to him if I spent a few months supervising the girls of Greystones, or working at some other profession, or doing nothing at all? Why not leave a chap the load of oof, as they say, and be done with it? Why blight his life by taking him away from the London season and sending him off to the seaside, where he might die of tedium?

Lizzie! Lizzie! How I wronged the frisky old fellow! Had I known what was to befall me at Greystones, I might almost have heard his laughter ringing out in the celestial spheres at my fury.

Fifty sovereigns was forwarded by old Silas Raven to see me safe to Pinebourne-on-Sea. Next morning, I received a letter from the Directress of Greystones, known to one and all as Miss Martinet. I was expected on the following Monday. The dogcart would be sent to the station to meet the three o'clock train.

Pinned to the letter was a list of useful clothing, including riding apparel for supervising the equestrian discipline of the girls. A further note, which made my brows rise slightly, referred to "instruments of correction." Such implements were provided by Miss Martinet for her colleagues. However, if I possessed a particular type of cane, birch, or whip, and if I preferred to use this, I might bring it with me. Naturally, the note added, it must be inspected and approved before I was authorised to use it on the bare bottom of any delinquent young woman.

I very nearly choked to death on my breakfast toast. With great care, I re-read the sentence. The words were still there—"bare bottom"—I had not fallen victim to hallucinations after all.

That was Saturday morning. Already my regrets at being parted from the London season were diminishing, and it seemed to me that Monday could not come soon enough. Believe me, Lizzie, it was not the thought of tanning the bare backside of a schoolgirl of fourteen or a runaway young wife of twenty-five which thrilled me. I was possessed by thoughts of what else might happen once I was privileged to see them slip their knickers down and pose for me.

By noon on Monday my bags were packed and secured, all my possessions crammed into them, as I waited with impatience for the cab that was to take me to Victoria. The half-past-twelve train was prompt to the minute. Seated in the dining car, I watched the houses of Pimlico and Balham speed past. Soon we were out in the countryside of Croydon and Purley, trees and hedges flashing by.

By breaking into old Silas Raven's fifty sovs, I sported a bottle of Chateau Rothschild and a first-rate spread. I sniffed my post-prandial brnady and smoked a cigar as we pulled in towards Lewes under the graceful curve of the Sussex downs. By three o'clock I stood on the platform at Pinebourne, breathing in the clean sharp air of the sea, which lay just beyond the town.

I knew Miss Martinet at first glance. She was quite tall, and smartly dressed with a look which one calls "handsome." Nearer thirty-five than forty, she wore her brown hair in a somewhat old-fashioned coiffure. Her manner was well educated and pleasant. She might equally well have been a young widow or, as proved to be the case, a lively minded spinster with a predilection for bending wayward young women to her will.

We drove together in the dogcart, exchanging pleasantries. Pinebourne was an agreeable place, I supposed, with its tree-lined shopping streets and its elegant, broad-paved Marine Parade. The freshly painted pier, the bandstand, the ornamental gardens with their yellow blooms in flower, lay beside a quiescent sea.

Would you imagine Greystones as some grim fortress of vengeance, Lizzie? How wrong you would be! Though surrounded by a high wall, which the nimblest damsel would never scale, the house and grounds were delightful. The house itself accommodated thirty penitent Magdalens, as old Silas Raven might call them, though their misdemeanours were more varied than the term implies. This extensive villa was light and airy, fronting onto ornamental grounds. Beyond the kitchen gardens at the rear stood the stable block with its little clock tower. To one side of the grounds rose the smooth turf of the downs, whose cliffs fell sheer to the tide. On the other side there was a gentle slope, where the resinous smells of warm pine led down to the rippling waters of the bay.

I took tea with Miss Martinet, who, because of my uncle's charitable interest in Greystones, treated me more as a guest than as an employee. Presently, however, she began upon one subject which had already crossed my own mind.

"You will find," said she, "that in such a place as this there are certain romantic passions which develop between some of the girls. A few of these are genuine affections, others are basely criminal. I cannot advise you whether to permit or punish such infatuations. It must be at your discretion. Whatever your decision, you may depend upon my support."

"I shall be grateful for that, ma'am," I said, swallowing my tea hard. The cup rattled nervously in the saucer, as I sat on the edge of the little chair in her drawing-room.

"Some girls," she continued, rather self-consciously, "are also liable to develop crushes or passions upon any man in the establishment. You, I am sure, will best know how to deal with that. They are also given to inventing stories about his activities. Have no fear, though, your word in such matters will always prevail with me."

"I shall strive to be worthy of such trust," I gasped weakly.

"As for the other matter," she murmured, "whatever course of action you feel to be necessary in matters of chastisement must be a decision for you alone."

As she spoke, Miss Martinet looked at me across the tea table with a new depth of meaning in her clear grey eyes. "I shall not interfere with your wishes in the matter," she went on, "except to assure you that the use of the rod is, paradoxically, the kindest form of correction in the end. A single severe punishment may save a wayward young woman from evil ways and repeated penalties later on."

"I'm obliged, ma'am," says I, awkwardly, "deuced obliged for that."

Miss Martinet smiled kindly at me. "Then we understand one another," she said quietly. "I knew that if your Uncle Brandon chose you as his heir he was certain that you would fit in with our way of doing things at Greystones."

Now, Lizzie, it may be that Miss Martinet understood, as she put it. I'll be damned if I did! Still I sensed, don't you see, some good sport ahead—just the kind that you and I love to hear of! Beyond the lace curtains of her upstairs drawing-room, the sun shone upon waves that were green as glass. Distantly, from the bandstand on the Marine Parade, came sounds of regimental brass.

"Tomorrow morning," said Miss Martinet, "you shall make your inspection. It was your uncle's wish that we should make you welcome here. I and the girls were, upon his instructions, to offer you every facility. Every facility." She looked at me, as she repeated those words, with that same depth of meaning which had made my heart beat faster a few moments before.

Ah, Lizzie! Tomorrow morning! What tales shall I have to tell you when I take up my pen tomorrow evening? For the present, as the lamp burns low, I bid you a loving goodnight and remain,

Your own adoring Charles

Greystones, 24 April 1904

My dearest Lizzie,

HOW DIFFERENTLY must we think of my Uncle Brandon after my adventures today! You might easily believe he had *owned* Greystones—Miss Martinet and the girls included—and that it was a private seraglio with Miss M. as a duenna!

After breakfast my hostess led me across the sun-lit lawns to the brick stable with its white cupola and clock. "We have two groups of girls at Greystones," she said proudly, "first, the more refined young ladies who are taught sewing or embroidery, and second, the young women trained to be stable-girls."

"Oh, aye," says I to myself, "buxom young trollops well made for vigorous riding and saddle work!"

"Before you proceed to deal with our young ladies," went on Miss M., "you must first prove yourself with these saucy Amazons. That was always your uncle's rule."

"Was it, by Jove!" I said. "Then I shall strive to be worthy of it!"

To speak well of Uncle Brandon is to win Miss M.'s heart. Do you suppose, my sweet, that she had such a lech for the old fellow as to supply him with young fillies to ride at Greystones?

"I shall put two young women in your charge at first—Maggie and Noreen," said she. "They need nothing less than a man's absolute authority. For that reason, your dear departed uncle wished you to aid our good works."

I smiled at the old fellow's singular notion of good works. A moment more and we entered the main stable door, viewing a well-kept interior of red tiling, white-painted rails, and neatly piled straw. Miss Martinet pointed out Maggie and Noreen to me, marking the beginning of my remarkable acquaintance with them.

I will not burden you with more than the briefest description of the two girls. Maggie was to prove a casual and careless young slut compared with the staring insolence of Noreen. What shall I say of Maggie? Her golden-blond hair hung straight and loose to her shoulders and was parted on her forehead in a long fringe. She was twenty-three years old, I learnt, the pale oval of her face marked by features which were firm and perhaps a little crude. Yet you would admire her blue-green eyes and the lashes which she darkens so skillfully. Maggie is a bewitching combination of the brazen slut and the innocent child. She is firmly built, though not tall. Her lack of height gives her a coltish, almost stocky appearance. Yet her thighs are taut and her hips firmly covered without being fat. Her breasts are softly hung and Maggie's bottom-cheeks have the trim maturity of womanhood. Though she wears no wedding ring, I'll wager that Maggie's cunt has been well ridden.

Noreen, by contrast, has an impudent stare and a resentful manner. This pleases me, rather, for it will offer ample pretext for discipline! Noreen is a trollop of nineteen with no claim to refinement. Would you picture her to yourself? You may do so easily. Imagine quite a tall, firmly made girl, her dark-brown hair worn straight and lank to the level of her collar and cut in a level fringe on her forehead. Add to this a set of strong, fair-skinned features and brown eyes of lazy malevolence. Men who like a well-made filly to strap between the shafts of love's chariot would stiffen at the sight of Noreen in her tight working pants and singlet. Firm young breasts and straight back are damply outlined by clinging blue cotton. Now observe her from the waist down: her belly is quite flat, her pubic mound a gentle swell. Her thighs are taut and lightly muscled, as if from work or exercise. Noreen's bottom is certainly quite big-cheeked but without any surplus fat.

"Deal firmly with them, Mr. Charles!" said Miss Martinet softly. "Be worthy of your Uncle Brandon! Remember, you are absolute master here. Not a word shall be heard against you from these girls!"

There were two grooms and several stable-boys to assist me in my task, which seemed to be no more than doing as I liked with the two girls! A room had been set apart for me at one end of the stable, and it was well appointed with a humidor of cigars and a decanter of fluid which looked, smelt, and tasted like the finest old malt! From this point of vantage, I settled down to watch Maggie through the open door.

The young blonde was laying out the saddle harness for inspection by the grooms. In doing this she was also in the public view. On that side the stable wall is the boundary of the Greystones estates, the

windows looking out onto the road, though securely
set in stone and not to be opened. Men and women
who stroll past can watch Maggie at work.

Perhaps it was this which made Maggie such an
exhibitionist. First she found a black wig in a cupboard and fitted it over her own blond hair. It was
not an improvement, though she paraded in it, her
jaw slack and her tongue running on her lips. Taking
it off at length, she ducked her head and shook it to
and fro vigorously, her blond hair flying then settling
at last into place.

The stable lads began to play with her. "Want a
good gallop, Mag?" they called, as they seized her.
"Take your pants right down, then!" She replied to
them banteringly in a voice which was surprisingly
soft and lilting. She tried to escape by climbing over
the harness rail. Her legs were too short and the boys
caught her as she was astride it. One gripped her
wrists and pulled her down so that she was lying forward along it as she straddled.

All this was done in play, Lizzie. Yet you may
imagine the faces of the men who were passing by
and who now pressed close to the windows to observe these proceedings. Because Maggie lay forward, astride the rail, the men outside the window
could stare at the weight of the soft young breasts
hanging like delectable fruit in her tight, blue singlet.
The wooden rail showed her pouched love-lips
through the straining tightness of her denim trousers.
Taut but maturely filled out, the firm cheeks of
Maggie's backside faced these spectators. There was
such wrestling between her and the stable-lads! One
of them stole a kiss from her lips, another smacked
her arse playfully several times through the tight,
thin denim.

In the end it was Maggie who freed herself. Then,

chewing insolently upon some sweetmeat in her mouth, she went to the stable-boy who was her favourite and took him by the hand. Now, it seemed, she was ready to pay any price for true love. She led the youth behind a screen which stood conveniently at one end of the stable. I heard the undoing of her waist and the whisper of Maggie's knickers being pushed down to her knees and then to her ankles.

"Lie down and let me play with it first, you wicked boy," she said teasingly in her soft Celtic lilt. "None of the schoolgirls can do it as well as I, can they?"

"Head to tail, Mag!" he gasped, "please! Let us lie head to tail!"

"Ah!" whispered Maggie, "you rascal! If I do that you will make me take it in my mouth!"

"Do it, Mag!" gasped the lad again, "do it all the same!"

His long sigh of contentment suggested that the coltish young blonde, with her curtains of light golden hair, had obeyed him in this matter.

"I must kiss you between the thighs, Maggie!" he murmured, "while my fingers stiffen those strawberry nipples on your white breasts. Was that nice when I kissed you there, Mag? Ah, how that makes you shudder—the tip of my tongue running in the love-slit between your thighs. Lie still, Maggie, and let me do it again. What a soft little cry! Anyone would think I had put you to the torture!"

I listened in stupefaction, my dearest Lizzie. Was this the way in which our English reformatories were run, I asked myself? Small wonder that such young whores as Maggie took their sentence with equanimity.

"Now your backside, Maggie!" sighed her adorer. "Did you see how the men admired you through the window each time they had a view from the rear as you bent over in your tight riding jeans? What would they like to do to you, Mag, if they had you as a slave girl? Suck softly, Maggie! Run your tongue about the cherry top! Now let me press your pale seat-cheeks apart and admire what lies between. Ah, yes, Maggie! If you were my slave girl, I should be pitiless in threading my shaft into that tight, dark hole as well. That frightens you a little? The thought of it makes you stiffen? To tell you the truth, Mag, the thought of it makes me stiffen too!"

So the lover's aria continued behind the stable screen. As I listened, I looked out across the green, sloping lawn towards the hedge which marked the steep fall of the cliff to the waves. It was the only side on which Greystones might seem unprotected. Yet no young damsel had ever been hardy enough to attempt a descent by that route. Nor, of course, had any randy swain ever managed to climb up by that way to woo his beloved in her reformatory bed! As I looked across the lawns and saw the pier and band-stand of Pinebourne glittering in the sun beyond, I could not help wondering what the respectable burghers of the town would feel if they knew the truth of the reformatory regime of which their law-makers were so proud.

Just then the grooms returned. Maggie, who had not nearly completed her chores, was sentenced to be chastised for her dilitoriness. When the first groom came to tell me that Maggie was made ready to be caned for idleness, I could hardly find an answer! Imagine how eagerly the men who had watched at the window while she worked at the harness display would have taken this opportunity! I could scarcely believe that it was my own voice saying, "Ah . . . yes . . . indeed. To be sure. Perhaps, though, on this first occasion, you would be good enough to deal with her for me."

A broad smile crossed the groom's face. All the passion which he had pumped into Maggie's mouth, the love with which he had spangled her thighs and backside, did not restrain his zeal for chastising her.

We went into the main part of the tiled stable, where a padded leather bench stood at the centre of the floor. Maggie was stripped to her singlet, made to kneel at one end of the bench and lie forward along it. Her discarded pants and knickers (a pair of stretched cotton briefs) lay discarded on the table. They had tied her blond hair in a short pony-tail, and I was pleased at that. It enabled me to watch more clearly her blue eyes and fair-skinned features.

I nodded to the groom, who made the preparations required by the Greystones regulations. Maggie's wrists were strapped to the far end of the bench, her waist buckled down, and her legs belted tightly together just above the knees.

All this will sound so severe, Lizzie, that you will scarcely credit how much pleasure there was for Maggie in her punishment. Yet such was the truth, as I discovered when I made my inspection of her before she was bamboo'd.

I squatted down behind her and studied the area which offered itself as a target to the groom. Maggie's buttocks, firmly and fully presented by her posture, were stretched hard apart. Both the rear pout of her vaginal purse and her anal cleft were in full view. I teased our blond shopgirl gently. "You've been making love, haven't you, Maggie?" I stroked her down the length of her cleavage, between the fair-skinned sturdiness of her buttocks, tickling the rear of her vaginal pouch and finding it moist. She was far away by now, her mouth open a little, and her blue-green eyes blank, as if she could not hear.

Can you guess the truth, Lizzie? Any of the other shopgirls punished in this manner—Pat or Jennifer or the rest—would have trembled at the ordeal. Maggie, however, was a lover of that delight known to us as "Birch in the Boudoir." Even a prison caning was the occasion for her pleasure. It is true, is it not, that certain girls, like the slave, Janina or the Grecian nymph, Sarita, have found pleasure under the rod of their Turkish masters? Maggie was a worthy novice!

Already I could see that her pale, firm thighs, in all their stocky power, were squeezing rhythmically together. It was impossible to prevent, except by ordering her legs to be strapped apart. To tell you the truth, my curiosity was so great that I could not bear to do that.

"No wonder the men watched you as you set out the harness display, Maggie," said the first groom, "if you were misbehaving like that!"

But the young shopgirl had no shame, Lizzie! I vow she continued with the thigh-squeezing and the buttock-clenching as if she could not have stopped it for dear life.

The groom cut the air with a trial swish of his bamboo. Our young blonde masturbatrix stopped, frozen in a moment of apprehension, and then resumed her labours of self-love.

"Thirty strokes across your bare bottom, Maggie," I said softly, and I nodded to the groom to begin the punishment with the long supple bamboo.

How the first stroke of the cane rang out across the firm, pale cheeks of Maggie's bottom! She gasped, cried out, but never ceased to squeeze her love-lips hard between her thighs. Again the cane lashed across her seat, and again. She gave a soft cry but it was hard to say whether pain or pleasure drew it from her. The groom was quite pitiless with her. Believe me, any true disciplinarian who had watched Maggie displaying herself at the window would have approved that. Six times the cane raised a weal across the cheeks of Maggie's bottom—and twice across the backs of her thighs. She cried out with the hurt and with the pleasure of her own thigh-squeezing at the same time. In truth the vicious prison bamboo was a smarting agony across the bare cheeks of her backside. Only the swelling balloon of pleasure in her own lions enabled her to endure it with such insouciance.

After the first fifteen strokes, the groom handed the cane to his colleague for the rest.

"Almost at the summit of your climb, Maggie?" asked the second man. "I shall let you get there before I cane. Then fifteen wicked strokes across your backside, with no distractions!"

Mag cried out again, begging him to bamboo her in her present state. But he waited until her thighs seemed to beat quickly in their squeezing, like soft white wings. He stood, undid her legs, and strapped them again with knees wide apart. Then he caned the impudent blonde shopgirl without compunction.

I was conscious that the lads she had romped with earlier had their eyes pressed to every chink and keyhole in the place. Under the second groom's attentions, Maggie screamed and her green eyes brimmed over. Unlike his predecessor, he was a moralist and no libertine. His righteous anger brought thin ruby trickles from the new weals across her bottom-cheeks.

At last Maggie lay limp and gasping, her behind blushing and marked by swollen stripes. I stroked her blond hair, calming her. "Come to my room tomorrow morning, Maggie," I said gently. "You'll be tanned now until the grooms are satisfied with you. Tomorrow, I'll treat you to some softer discipline of my own."

Was it pleading or was it gratitude she showed? Maggie, the randy young bitch, brazenly licked my fingers in anticipation! Had she much to be grateful for? It depends which groom was the harder to satisfy. Was she given to the gentler of the two? He would surely allow her to ride the rubber dildo while his rod merely stimulated her passion. But Maggie the young shopgirl with her golden-blond hair touching her collar and fringed on her forehead, might well provoke a gentle, affectionate lechery.

Yet the other groom seemed more fiercely provoked. Was it by the rather hard, crude features in the pale oval of her face, or the blue-green eyes with their mascara'd lashes? Did her slight stockiness, the firm young thighs and buttocks, move him even more?

With the first lover, Maggie might play out an amorous comedy. If the second was allowed to take her into the fateful room, a darker drama would ensue. It represents a more sombre scene, shadows falling on a fixed block where Maggie kneels strapped over it, securely gagged. Only her short, black singlet clothes her. I fear the tale must be one of Maggie's wadded screams and flooding tears, her bottom bruised and swollen by weals which will not fade for a week. Even then, I suspect, this wielder of the pony-switch knows no pity.

I wonder which of my suppositions is correct? Perhaps neither. Perhaps, indeed, I malign the second fellow. Yet there was a certain look in his eye. Not that I think him alone in his inclinations towards such a young woman as Mag!

Now, my dearest Lizzie, I send this, my second letter, to you. As of this moment, you will not have received one. But, when you do, how sweet your replies will be to your own adoring,

Charles

Greystones, 28 April 1904

My own Lizzie,

*W*HAT A FOOL! What a fool he is,
I hear you say. To procure such pleasure for Maggie
and her admirers, but never to taste it for himself.
Believe me, my dearest, you could not think worse of
me than I did myself in that respect. I groaned all
night at my folly in having let slip the opportunity to
enjoy an evening with Maggie. It shall not happen
again, I said to myself. For now it was clear that I
was lord and master of the young women whom
Miss Martinet—or rather my Uncle Brandon—had
provided for me. I could do *anything* I chose, to
whatever girl I chose.

Now the trouble about that state of affairs is that
it rather spoils a fellow for choice. I might have
spent the next six months making up my mind and
changing it again. If there was one young woman
who unwittingly saved me from this, she was Noreen.

Yesterday, after two days of remorse and indeci-
sion, I went down to the stable-block again. The harness had been polished, and Noreen was rubbing up

the tiles with a damp cloth, toiling away in her white singlet and working trousers.

Picture her, Lizzie! A firmly made, quite tall girl of nineteen. Unlike Maggie's easy sluttiness, there was a hard defiance in Noreen's clear, pale features and insolent brown eyes. The dark-brown hair, cut at the collar, fell about her face as she knelt there polishing. From time to time, she flicked her fringe and shook the straight, dark hair into place.

You may be sure that the passers-by on the path were detained by the sight of her. What did they see? A firm-figured young trollop in clothes so snug-fitting that you might imagine her naked! The singlet, as she knelt on hands and knees, shaped the taut, young breasts, which nevertheless jiggled nicely with the vigour of rubbing the tiles. The tight, pale-blue denim of her pants moulded those long, lightly muscled thighs, so trim that, when she was on all fours, with knees pressed together, there was a little space and light between those taut limbs. Her hips in this pose were perhaps her greatest attraction for the voyeurs, Noreen's behind being quite big-cheeked without running to fat.

The harness strap round her waist, serving to keep the pants in place, pulled them tight over Noreen's robust young buttocks. As she worked, the central jeans seam was strained like a hawser deep between the cheeks of Noreen's bottom and under her legs. The softer, fuller swell of her lower bum-cheeks almost closed over it. Yet it remained visible, the tight denim showing how the seam even parted the lips of Noreen's vagina.

Indignant at her unwanted admirers, she shook her hair back and looked coldly 'round at them, stopping her work, posing immobile on all fours. The silk-hatted gentlemen smiled eagerly at her, tongues running over their lips. She sat back on her heels, refusing to oblige them any longer. The groom came over to her.

"Noreen, you young slattern! To your work at once! Unless you would prefer the gentlemen to see you reprimanded!"

I confess, Lizzie, my tool began to stiffen both at the sight of Noreen and the thought of training her for my pleasure. In short, I gave instructions that she and another young woman were to attend me in my room. Need I tell you? She resisted every advance. Her face was turned away from my kisses. I had intended first to make Noreen suck my penis, kneeling before me, prior to swiving her cunt soundly. Her defiance was such that I feared she might bite clean through it! She could be won, but she must first repent of her hostility. Without further ado, the grooms laid her on the bed, with its leather wristlets secure to the frame at the head. If she had no taste for love, she should not interrupt others.

My second companion could only be Maggie. This young blond slut with her coltish stockiness stood there waiting, tongue pressed between teeth. She had hauled up the front of her singlet and was running a hand over her belly as if to check that its shape had not been spoilt. For the rest, she wore the same blue working jeans as all the other girls during their labours in the stable, where there is no place for skirts and petticoats.

Even Noreen could not help watching Maggie undress. That was odd, Lizzie. I vow the two girls must often have watched each other disrobe. To prevent solitary vice in such places as Greystones, bath hours and toilet visits are shared by at least two young women, as a rule. Will you confess the truth? To see a girl undress fascinates women as much as men!

I drew a chair close to the bed, where Noreen lay and removed my trousers, displaying the erection which had been longing for liberty. Both girls turned their eyes upon it as I sat down. Maggie came close, shifted her firm, white thighs apart, and seemed to know what to do.

"Astride my legs, Maggie, facing me! I want to sheathe myself very deeply between your legs. We shall let Noreen drool over the chance she has missed. And you'll be well positioned for me to enjoy your lips and breasts, to play with your legs and arse."

Maggie looked at me, hard and lascivious, as she moved her thighs wider yet and clambered astride me. Lowering her hips she touched the knob with her hole as if by instinct. I put a hand under her and smiled at the amount of self-lubrication.

"You young whore, Maggie! You've been making love to yourself!"

"What if I have?" She shook her blond fringe with a hardened impudence.

"Would you like to be made to do it in front of the men who admired you while you were setting out the harness?"

"Don't mind."

I'm sure she did mind, but Mag was too brazen to admit it. I turned her 'round a moment and was not the least surprised by the fading traces of stripes and one or two small bruises on Maggie's bottom-cheeks. It was clear that, when I left after her punishment the other night, one of the grooms had taken Maggie into another room and caned her viciously.

"Very well, Maggie," I said quietly, "the next time you're caught at it, I'll have you strapped for the pony-lash on your bare bottom. How do you like the prospect of that?"

For answer, Maggie gave a little hip swagger and impaled herself astride me! She is more of a slut than her friends Jenny and Pat, but deliciously lewd as well. She thrust her tongue into my mouth and began to ride the erection.

"You randy young bitch, Mag!" I gasped. "I believe you really were trying to show yourself to all the men who passed by!"

Her cunt was tight and smooth, exquisitely so. As I rode to bursting point I also tasted the fresh mint in her saliva.

"I'm going to come," she whispered soon. "I've been on heat all day for this. I can't help it. Let me do it harder!"

Her juice seemed to be streaming down over my cock already, but that was mere lubrication. She pulled up the singlet so that I could smooth her belly with one hand and worry her nipples with my teeth. I kissed her forehead, where the blond fringe parted. With my free hand I fingered her arsehole.

"You won't be spared that way either, Maggie! If we have to strap you bending for the lash, the stable-boys won't be able to resist it! Remember that when next you play with yourself!"

Mag is one of those girls who are excited by violent imaginings. I murmured promises in her ears of places where she might be taken and given to the unspeakable lusts of libertines. She cried out in her triumph, her head hanging limply over my shoulder, her hair loose down my back. Shuddering, she went into one erotic spasm after another. Her screams, which might have been pleasure or torment, decreased at last, and she flopped almost senseless against me. Kissing her eyes I tasted tears of relief—or even frustration. Then I comforted her for she was sobbing quietly in the reaction from such exultation. I kissed her gently on the nipples, on the belly, on the warm, firm cheeks of her bum, and then on the lips again. I led her gently to the sofa and bade her lie there.

"You will rest a little, Maggie," I said, smiling at her. "You must gather all your strength again for the night which lies before us. Ah, I see a tear or two in the desolation which follows such joy! Have no fear, you shall scale the summit of pleasure again in a little while!"

I crossed the room to the bed, where Noreen lay. She was able to gaze her fill on the stiff, sinewy tool, which had lost none of its sap in the recent engagement with Maggie. Yet Noreen's firm, pale features were a study in vulgar indifference. She merely shook into place the level fringe of the brown hair, whose tresses brushed her collar.

Walking 'round the bed, I sat down on the far side. Because Noreen's wrists were held together at the far corner of the head-rail, she bent forward from the waist as she lay there on her side. She watched me over her shoulder, still with the same dismissive indifference. Because she was curved forward on her side, her seat was presented to me in the most suggestive manner. Even now she was still garbed in her stable costume of white singlet and tight, pale-blue riding jeans. The broad leather belt pulled her pants taut, the denim stretched smooth over her firm, full buttocks. I stroked these two provoking mounds lightly and returned her gaze.

"I should very much like to give you a good caning tonight, Noreen. Your conduct certainly merits it. Unfortunately, the rules require me to enter it in the book first. I shall do so in the morning. In a week's time you will learn the bitter lesson of bamboo."

I said this without intending to carry out the threat just then, for I wished to see what effect the menace would have. I might have saved my breath, for she maintained the same stolid stare. Slowly I drew my finger down the stout central seam of her jeans seat. The seam was drawn deep and taut between her bottom-cheeks, their lower fatness gently closing over it, then it strained under her legs, almost running between the lips of her cunt, whose shape appeared as a soft swell. For the first time, the hard impudent stare faltered.

"You must mend your manners a little," I said. "The next time that men choose to admire you, show yourself thankful for their flattery. Life will be hard for you otherwise."

She shook her fringe again. "What are you going to do to me?" Her first words were spoken grudgingly.

"Little as you deserve it, Noreen, you shall receive love's elixir inside you."

She looked uneasy at this, for she feared a swollen belly more than anything else.

"Have no fear," I said, it will be in a place where no babies are conceived."

My open hand was now smoothing lightly over her strapping young seat. As the meaning of this penetrated, she made a show of protesting vigorously.

"Don't be foolish, Noreen. I'm sure something quite as large has often passed that way."

By now I was undoing her belt and easing her pants down to her knees. A moment more, and I was able to admire in their perfect nudity the hard-exercised young thighs and the well-made cheeks of Noreen's bottom.

"You have yourself to blame," I said gently. "By

refusing the offer at first, you have earned second-best. Be a sensible girl and accept what must be. Perhaps you will then enjoy it more readily."

I had no doubt that she was more than ready to accept the same tribute as her companion. But I vowed to myself she must not expect to refuse and demand so willfully. My hands fondled her firmly feminine thighs for a moment. Then my fingers played capriciously with her nineteen-year-old seat, running over the cheeks and between them. She opened her legs a little.

"Do it this way."

"Certainly not," I said. "Apart from the risk of what might follow, you have already refused that offer. I shall not ask again until your repentance is quite sure."

Noreen's backside, though big-cheeked, was not flabby, yet there was a fatter softness just above her thighs. Pressing her pale buttocks apart with my hands, I pondered the tight inward dimple, so perfectly made. I stroked her seat-cheeks lightly.

"You're very well made for it in that area, aren't you, Noreen? I can scarcely believe this is the first time."

Opening a jar, I lubricated my fingers and vase-lined Noreen between her buttocks. Then, to her surprise I got up.

"Do it!" she said breathlessly, in her uneasy anticipation. "Do it now!"

"Lie there like that and wait, Noreen. You'll be well rewarded when I'm ready. You must learn that such love-making as goes on in this room will last all night. I pity the man who marries you if he is only to get a few moments of quick frantic excitement and then no more."

So I went across to Maggie, who lay facing us

with her hands clasped between her legs. She was gently and wistfully playing with herself. I helped her to turn over so that I could then compare the young blonde's rear anatomy with that of her companion. Like Noreen, she shook back her fringe and watched me.

"Will you be ready for love's hammerhead to knock at so tight a portal, Maggie?" I asked gently. "I wonder how you will respond when the time comes?"

You may easily imagine the response from Maggie, with her rather crude, hard features, her slack and sluttish manner. She shook her blond fringe again in order to turn her head farther and kiss the knob of my tool.

All this time, Noreen lay in rising apprehension at what was in store for her. "Do it now," she implored, trying to twist her rump round in our direction, "please!"

Here was a change indeed! Like a schoolgirl who knows she must have the birch, Noreen could endure the ordeal itself more readily than the agony of waiting. She wanted it to happen so that it would be over. And yet she dreaded it happening at all!

Ignoring her, I allowed Maggie to close her mouth over the knob and its shaft, but I forbad her to do more for fear of precipitating a deluge. What a hardened young slut she is! Small wonder that the gentlemen who witnessed her setting out the harness display had been so entranced!

"Play with yourself at the same time, Maggie!" I said, teasingly, and the blonde girl obeyed at once.

It was some while before I went back to Noreen. Sitting down on the far side of the bed again, I touched her where she was so well prepared. "Is that the worst of it, Noreen? Wondering what it will be like—Will you be hurt by it? Will you enjoy it? Will it disgust you or excite you? Perhaps all those things will happen—and perhaps not!"

I stretched myself out, covering her from the back so that I could adjust my knob to her tight rear dimple. I pressed apart the pale Amazonian cheeks of Noreen's bottom. Love's hammerhead knocked for admission in earnest, yet it was not easy at first to make headway. The knob would lodge in Noreen's anus and then find an invincible tightness.

"Open yourself for it, Noreen," I said gently, "or will nothing short of a good spanking put you in the mood?"

She hesitated then. Drawing back, I circled her waist with my left arm. My right hand fell in a series of explosive smacks on each of Noreen's bum-cheeks in turn. I gave her a dozen well-measured stingers on each. Though it was only with my hand, she was tensing and shifting her arse desperately by the end, drawing her breath in wild gasps.

"There are young ladies who cannot abandon themselves to their lovers without a tanning to drive the modesty from them, Noreen," I said. "Can that truly be the case with such a young trollop as you? Are you secretly eager for the prick while your heart demands the pretext of being whipped into submission?"

I made her keep her head turned so that I could admire her features and the dark fringe of her hair. I now kissed her on the mouth and touched the knob to the dimple again. This time I felt Noreen's arsehole swell as if trying to open for me. My kiss upon her mouth muffled her shrillness as I went forward with all my resolve. The tight buttonhole yielded and I passed through the exquisitely narrow portals to my great pleasure.

"The full length of it up your behind now, Noreen," I said softly, and gave it her in one long steady plunge. With what alarm she cried out, feeling it so deeply, swearing that she could locate the sensation of the knob in her bellybutton.

"Turn over on your front a little more, Noreen," I said, trying to reassure her. "Let me slide a hand under your bare belly to support you there while I bugger you. Good. So responsive to the penis inside you? I believe you find some enjoyment in it already!"

Having turned her over a little, I found that Noreen wanted to arch her rump out more fully to ease the burden of the phallus. By good fortune, this enabled me to push even farther into her.

"Noreen, my love," my lips touched her ear. "Keep your face turned to me. That's better. Now join in the rhythm of delight."

I pulled her singlet hem well up so that I could look down and watch my erection plunging in and out between the pale cheeks of her bottom, her rear muscle stretched round its hard circumference. I rode with a firm, slow thrust while she lay there, still and tense. As the minutes passed, however, the shape of the penis naturally began to stimulate certain excitements in her, however unhealthy they might have been. There was a certain slight muscular movement. I caught her eye at this.

"Still too timid, Noreen? Are you afraid that you might damage yourself if you give your feelings free play? I can promise you that you will enjoy it much more if you join in the dance!"

And so she did, her seat rising to meet my thrusts and then drawing away slightly at the withdrawal. She begged me for a libation to be poured out quickly. I felt her anus tighten in small exciting movements on my shaft.

"We must not hurry our pleasures, Noreen," I said. Did I detect alarm or excitement in her brown eyes at this? After ten minutes I stilled her and made her lie quietly with my tool embedded while passion came off the boil. Then I allowed her to begin again. At last I could be denied no longer. For safety's sake I made her lie still and I steadied her with a hand each side of her hips.

"A vigorous finish now, Noreen," I said, smiling at her and brushing her straight, dark hair back to see her face. She was lying with the edge of the pillow clenched between her teeth! With long strokes I began to pump and suck the narrow way of her behind with my tool. I pressed the pale mounds of her backside hard apart, so that I might plunge farther and make her feel the explosion of lust as deeply within her bottom as was possible. She caught her breath several times as I touched one area then another of profound sensitivity.

"Do you want to feel the sperm in your behind now, Noreen?"

She nodded her head vigorously, without releasing the pillow between her teeth.

"Very well, you young slut!" My own teeth were set now in my passion. "The first squirt of it deep in your arse, Noreen! Ah! Does that make you quiver? Again! Noreen, my love! How I shall flood your young backside! There! And there! You young whore, Noreen! Delicious young whore! Ah! Tighten on the shaft again! Delectable! Noreen! Ah, Noreen! Noreen, darling!"

With passion spent, I allowed her gently to squeeze my tool from her bottom with slight muscular movements. Its weight lolled softly across her broad, pale seat-cheeks, leaving a final trail of passion. Then I lay there to recuperate.

I was busy with Maggie an hour later. This young, blond minx, with her firm stocky build, had quite enthralled me. Maggie was on her back, knees pulled up, legs wide, while I rode into her young cunt with renewed vigour. Noreen had, not unnaturally, been permitted to visit the stable closet. I was still toiling at Maggie when the other girl returned.

Maggie shook her blond fringe—a gesture like Noreen's—and turned her face from me, watching the other bed.

"Mag, you young bitch!" I said crossly, "pay attention to what I'm doing to you!"

She ran her tongue round her teeth in a suggestion of humour and looked away again.

"Look at her, then!" Mag whispered, in her light, lilting voice.

Noreen was lying on her side, half of her belly, in the familiar pose. What had Maggie seen? I disengaged, went across, and looked. What do you think? The sturdy cheeks of Noreen's bottom blushed deeply. Here and there they bore the muddy imprint of the hard rubber heel of a canvas gymnastic slipper. I could scarcely understand it. Could it be that, while she was in the toilet closet, Noreen had persuaded someone—a groom or even a stable-lad—to tan her hard with a gym-shoe? Either the heel was damp or had been spat upon for greater effect.

Maggie was standing beside me now. "Don't you see?" she murmured, "that's to say how sorry she is. Isn't it, Nor?"

Believe me, neither of those two girls left that same bed during the rest of the night. Mag sucked again first, then Noreen. Next I spread Noreen's legs

and brought her to dumb ecstasy. After that I would
have been envied by some of those who admired
Mag's nicely rounded arse-cheeks as she bent in the
stable room. Turning her over, one hand under her
belly to support her, I spread Maggie's bottom-
cheeks and buggered her in turn. The blond hair was
presented to me, but the mirror showed her face, the
hard pale features and predatory blue eyes under her
fringe. I guessed it was not her first time.

You will believe me, dearest Lizzie, when I tell
you that the early summer dawn lightened the gardens outside before our pleasures were concluded.
Indeed, my letter was begun immediately I came
back to my rooms in the house itself, and is now finished as the maid brings in my breakfast.

Will you be too jealous if I tell you that the maid
is Maggie and that there is a note on the tray from
Miss Martinet? On the breakfast tray there also lies
a slim bamboo. My left hand, the one with which I
do not write, guides Maggie to bend over the desk.
She turns her head aside, the collar-length hair too.
Such a hard and knowing young face with its pale
oval and its darkly made-up blue eyes. The well-
formed, tightly-rounded cheeks of Maggie's arse are
so close I can scarcely move the pen. My hand
shapes them.

"Take down your pants, Maggie! Miss Martinet
orders you the cane!"

Now my hand fondles Mag's bare thighs and
backside. I really must break off, dearest. . . .

"Miss Martinet guessed I should enjoy this, Maggie! Bend right over the table while the straps are
drawn!"

. . . . And now, dearest, the sun is an hour
higher in the sky and I may resume. Maggie's bottom is a sight indeed. She kneels in repentance be-

fore me, her blond fringe tickling my bare belly, her tongue moistening her lips as she unbuttons nimbly.

Believe me, Lizzie, only my loss of you drives me to these wild resorts of passion! Such are the woes of the flesh!

Your own adoring Charles

Ramallah, 4 May 1904

My dearest Charlie,

FAITHFUL TO my promise, as
ever, I write by the first post for England to tell you
of the amusements which I have witnessed since our
arrival in this place. Alas, my sweet, we must be separated for weeks—perhaps months—but I vow I
shall entertain you with anything of a frisky nature
which comes my way. Thus you may know that your
adoring Lizzie still cares for you as fondly as ever,
and longs only to keep your spirits up and your resolve stiff until our next dear embraces.

How shall I begin! A few hours after our ship
docked, we were borne away in a regal carriage to
the residence which my father enjoys here as Britannia's ambassador. Cool, white-panelled rooms
awaited us behind a garden of palm trees and purple
bougainvillea. All is gilt and embossed, fit for the
king himself. And yet what tedium would this have
promised me—so much empty ceremonial and dull
diplomacy—had it not been for the kindness of the
Pasha of Ramallah.

The Pasha is a delightful companion, witty and courteous, always deferential to my rank and sensibilities as the daughter of a British envoy. He is a darkly handsome man of about forty, educated at the best schools in England and then at the Sorbonne. His house, overlooking the deep blue of the bay, is grand enough for a palace. Yet it is nothing to his country estate, some twenty miles away in a desert oasis, where he keeps his wealth and his harem.

Ah, you wicked boy! Do I sense that your ears prick up at the word "harem"? Come, I will not scold you! To speak the truth, I was so intrigued by the notion, that my longing to see the beautiful slave girls in their silken and perfumed prison of love was quite as strong as is your own. However, my dearest, I, as a mere woman, might hope to be admitted there. You, alas, never could.

At first, indeed, it seemed to me that even I should never manage to prompt an invitation from the Pasha to visit that private place. We were, of course, given a general invitation to visit the fine country house. Charlie, you never saw the like of it! The oasis is a green island in an ocean of brilliantly white desert sand. A high wall surrounds the place, and it is well guarded by his soldiers to keep marauders away. Inside are the most beautiful ornamental gardens with little hills, lakes, pahts, temples of delight, and the bright, perfumed flowers of Arabia.

What shall I say of the house itself? It is a place of marble courtyards and ornate fountains, colonnades of Moorish arches, like the Alhambra itself. The rooms are sometimes open and sunny, sometimes deep and mysteriously dark, the scent of burnt spice rising from the braziers. England knows nothing as rich as the secret world of bright silks and dark tapestries, the stools and sofas which seem made to shape a woman's body to her lover's commands.

However great my curiosity, I was careful not to show undue interest in the harem at first. I talked of it casually to the Pasha. Charlie! What do you think? He confessed to a taste for English and European girls as well as Arabian, Indian, and even Caribbean. I could not object to this, knowing that my father's power rendered me entirely safe. Yet my eagerness to see the beauties of his seraglio was now keener than ever. To my astonishment, he said casually, "If you are free to come on your own tomorrow, I shall order Nabyla to take you to the gallery from which you can view my treasures."

Can you doubt that I seized this opportunity at once? I was protected from harm by the position of my family and, even had this not been the case, my ravening curiosity would soon have conquered my misgivings. It is rare enough for a guest—man or woman—to see the beauties of the harem. What was still more provoking in this case was the knowledge that the Pasha of Ramallah had such a splendid collection of European odalisques as well as those of warmer climes.

Next afternoon, I was punctual to the minute. After the usual compliments had been exchanged, my host summoned a young Arabian beauty, Nabyla, who was to be my guide. She had a taut, swaggering voluptuousness of figure, skin like dark-gold satin, fiery eyes, and a sweep of silky black hair. In her company I was led to a gallery of white-and-black marble arches, rather like a cloister, which ran round one of the main rooms. Latticework filled the spaces of the archways so that we were able to spy upon the occupants without being seen ourselves.

Sunlight filtered through coloured glass high overhead, illuminating one of the Pasha's favourites. My guide explained to me in English that this was Tania, a girl of twenty, from the Pasha's European collection. I was taken at once by the soft prettiness of her face and figure, her rather short crop of brown curls clustered on her forehead. Such a pert female cherub, I thought, the nose neat and straight, the chin nicely tucked in. Her sun-kissed face has, I imagine, a delightful tendency to dimple when she smiles. As with most girls from that eastern clime, her cheekbones are high and her blue eyes shadowed by them.

As we observed her, Tania was by no means fully dressed. She boasted only a snug-fitting, white singlet and a pair of light-blue denim drawers, which were tight as skin from her waist to her knees. We came upon her in this charming costume just as she was stooping over a table, resting on her elbows, reading a book. What a delightful picture she made!

Her soft young breasts hung tantalisingly in the tight cotton of the singlet. You would agree, I know, that her young hips are quite broad. Best of all, she has a charming tendency when bending like this to hollow the back of her waist downward so that the broad young cheeks of her bottom appear well separated in their tight denim. She has the easy, lewd pose of an *immoraliste*, however proper her upbringing. With her hips slack, one knee bent at a time, she offers each cheek of her rump alternately.

I could not tell you, Charlie, what charming volume of curious literature she was reading. Yet its effect upon her was all too soon visible: her backside began to stir in a quiet rhythm as she bent over the table reading, and her thighs smoothed softly together in their tight knickers.

"You see how it is?" Nabyla said to me quietly.

"There are so many harem slave girls. There are such numerous girls here that a night of excitement in the Pasha's bed is rare—unless they are one of his great favourites. Yet that occasional exquisite ordeal of her master's tool is enough to stimulate the itch of lust in such girls. Worse still, they live in the luxury of idleness with nothing else to think about. For the master's delight, books of amorous tales are provided as their only reading. The mistress appointed to supervise them will inspect them so intimately each morning with her fingers that love's demands will plague them the rest of the day. Tania would prefer another girl to console herself with at the moment. In default of that, she will take matters into her own hands."

Her words were true to the last syllable. As we watched, Tania slipped one hand down between her tightly clad thighs and began to finger her own love-pouch.

"Tell me," I asked. "Tania's body is surely her master's absolute property by the law of the harem? Every function of it, I imagine, is his to command or forbid as he chooses?"

"Indeed," said Nabyla, gently.

"Then, if Tania masturbates without his consent, will that not be a fault to be reprimanded?"

Nabyla's dark eyes had a gleam of amusement in them as she turned her proud Arabian face to me. "That will depend, madam. There will be times when the Pasha wishes to take Tania's knickers down and give her a sound whipping. What better pretext than such misbehaviour as this? Yet at other times he will be delighted by her misconduct, either because it prepares her for his own pleasure or because he can then immediately oblige her to continue making love to herself as an amusement for his guests."

How intriguing this was, I thought! And what a new light it cast upon the amiable Pasha of Ramallah!

Tania looked about her, straightened up, and went across to the leather divan. No doubt she believed that she was quite undetected in her mischief. I think she was still very timid over the matter of being caught in such misbehaviour for, as yet, she did not even dare to take down her knickers. Instead, our young odalisque, with her crop of brown curls, lay on the divan, propped on her elbow. She turned slightly on her side away from us, crossing her legs very tightly and turning her broad young rump to our side with charming lasciviousness. Yet she had her shoulders turned so that we saw her face and the soft swell of breasts in her singlet.

I believe that Tania was looking over her shoulder because she feared that discovery might threaten on that side. At the same time, it was not possible for someone entering suddenly to see precisely what her hands were doing in front of her. For all that, there was never the least doubt in our minds what the young minx was up to!

Her thighs squeezed rhythmically together upon her busy finger. The broad young cheeks of Tania's arse pressed hard together and swelled out alternately. The blue eyes of the masturbatrix closed, fluttered open, then closed in a dream of bliss. Her luscious mouth opened softly to draw the deeper breaths which her rising excitement demanded. Her tongue ran repeatedly along her lips, moistening the dryness of love's fever.

Nabyla left me for a moment and I continued to watch Tania masturbate with the greatest interest. I vow to you, Charlie, that I had *never* been privileged to see another girl do this to herself. Young ladies of my acquaintance were, of course, known to practise such dark rituals—either alone or in couples—but to see this done was an experience I had never hoped for.

In a trice, Nabyla was back. She was accompanied by a rather severe-looking young woman whose name I learnt was Judi. Unlike the others, Judi was the Pasha's mistress—in the English sense—rather than his slave. She was also the mistress—in the harem sense—of some of his slave girls. Judi was no more than twenty-five, her blond hair strained back into a short plait. Her fine-boned face with its sharp features matched the description of her as Tania's mistress. She was appropriately dressed in riding breeches and shirt, carrying a short leather switch.

Tania was allowed to make love to herself for a little while until Judi at last opened a door and walked into the room. What do you think Tania did? What could she do? Drawing her hands clear of her love nest, she lay down on the divan and pretended to be asleep. As Judi went across to her, she appeared to stir from a light afternoon doze!

There was no doubt of Judi's authority, or of Tania's state of arousal. Tania's first act was to take Judi's free hand between her own, kissing its knuckles and gold rings as if these were the objects she loved most in the world. Then she held the blond woman's hand against her own face and nuzzled against it contentedly.

"Now," Judi said at last, "I fear we must satisfy the Pasha that you have been guilty of no act of wantonness, Tania!"

Tell me, Charlie, how do you suppose that was done? I wager you would never guess.

Tania lifted her hips obediently so that Judi could slip her knickers down and off. As I suspected,

Tania is one of those twenty-year-olds whose hips are broad and full without being flabby. Her thighs and bottom were what I would call fair-skinned, though perhaps a little muddy in their complexion. Presently she turned, holding and kissing Judi's hand again, showing the nice thatch of brown ringlets which adorns her pubis.

"Lie on your back, Tania!" said Judi sharply. "Bend your knees up to your breasts."

What was to happen now? Judi sat on the divan and looked down at Tania's vaginal pouch so conveniently presented by her new posture. Then, from a drawer, the blond mistress took a little tin and a badger-hair shaving-brush. Can you guess, even now, what was about to take place?

The tin contained a dry, white powder, a form of soap. In order to determine Tania's guilt or innocence of the act of masturbation, the dry powder was to be brushed into the suspected place by the soft teasing brush. If it lathered, then Tania was guilty. If, after several minutes, it did not, she was innocent.

One cannot quarrel with the ingenuity of such a procedure. Yet Judi had no intention of performing the ritual herself. She went to another door and called one of those slave girls who testify to the Pasha's universality of taste.

How shall I describe Shawn, eighteen years old? She is quite tall, a graceful Caribbean beauty with a high-boned facial beauty and tight-lidded slanted eyes. Her dark hair is strained back into a tight little bun or top-knot held in place by a tortoise-shell comb. This coiffure not only enables one to enjoy the fineness of her features more easily but gives an air of charming dignity to this tawny-skinned Venus.

Shawn was also in *déshabillé*, in a bright-yellow cotton tunic, belted at the waist, and ending at mid-thigh. She was, I later heard, much given to dressing up in various costumes and admiring her reflection in the long mirrors of the harem *baignoire*.

Before leaving the two girls together, Judi positioned Tania's wrists above the young woman's head, by the ring at the end of the leather divan. Then the blond mistress joined us so that she might watch the results of her preparations.

Shawn was in no hurry, it seemed. She stood before a mirror, adjusting the yellow tunic dress. The firm, coffee-skinned elegance of her long legs, bare to mid-thigh, was admirable. The tight skirt of the short, yellow dress strained and creased easily across her lithe hips and the taut statuesque cheeks of her bottom.

At last she was ready, turning to her willing victim. You will easily imagine Shawn dipping the brush in the powdered soap and applying it to Tania's nether lips. But will you guess how she did it? She knelt astride Tania, almost sitting on the girl's breasts, facing her feet. Then she went forward on elbows and knees, her face above the open spread of Tania's crotch, as she tickled the powder-laden brush into Tania's cunt. Tania moaned and sobbed gently with the delicious torment of it. Our tall, agile Caribbean beauty smiled to herself at this, teasing the tip of the brush 'round and 'round Tania's clitoris. At the same time, the tormentress reached back and pulled her own tight, yellow dress up above her waist. What a view was now presented to Tania's eyes and lips!

Under so short a tunic, Shawn's knickers were a pair of white ballet briefs made of stretched cotton web. What a contrast they made with the smooth coffee colour of her long, agile thighs. She has that natural Caribbean grace of the straight back and

long trim legs, the instinctively upright carriage. Her
hips are firm, though offering a slightly fuller appeal
than the rest of her figure, her breasts being high
and saucy. The tight, white cotton of the briefs perfectly shaped the triangle of her pubis and showed
the charming little bulge of her love-pouch through
their gusset. She had chosen a pair which were cut
lasciviously high and tight at the seat, laying bare
much of the soft, dusky-gold cheeks of her backside.

Inspecting Tania's furry pouch at very close
range, Shawn tickled it pitilessly with the brush,
touching and teasing, touching and teasing, until
Tania's blue eyes widened and she cried out, her
brown curls threshing from side to side on the divan.
Shawn moved her knees back a little so that she was
astride Tania's face. All the time she was manipulat-
ing the little brush with wicked skill, teasing and
touching, teasing again and again.

To be masturbated in this fashion was almost
more than Tania could bear without going into a delirium of screams and pleading. She kissed the in-
sides of Shawn's nude thighs with an amorous,
smacking passion. Then her tongue began to lick the
soft, satiny inner surfaces of the thighs with long, in-
fatuated swathes of moisture.

Shawn was smiling to herself as the brush continued its work on Tania's vagina. The result of the test
was no longer in doubt for we could hear the first
faint whisper of lather at Tania's own love-juice sup-
plied the powder with ample moistening.

"Pull your pants down, Shawn," she whispered
yearningly, "oh, please do, my dearest! Let me love
you properly!"

I think the Caribbean beauty was perhaps more
amused than flattered by the grand passion she had
provoked. Yet Tania was now desperately kissing the

tight, warm cotton where it cuddled the soft little bulge of Shawn's vaginal pouch. At this rate, I thought, she was soon going to taste Shawn through the pants in any case.

As it happened, the generous girl obliged her. Shawn reached back, took the waistband of her knickers and pulled them down so that they were drawn tight round the middle of her spread thighs. Now the two girls lay on their sides, head to tail, facing one another for a prolonged session of love-making.

Shawn began remorselessly working her finger in and out of Tania's love-hole, causing cries of gratitude and alarm from her soft-figured partner. It was Shawn who was the leader, quite shameless in her wanton use of the other girl. Her tongue now replaced her finger in Tania's little slit, trilling like that of an exotic bird in full song. Tania, for her part, was content to obey Shawn's instructions, kissing and tonguing according to order. Because her wrists had been placed out of harm's way by her mistress, she needed a little assistance from her partner. Shawn, ravaging Tania with her tongue, had to reach back and part her own buttocks so that Tania might more deeply explore her in that area.

Presently I saw that Tania's hips were moving in a hard, pumping kind of motion. She was about to have her "happy time," as they call it in French parlance. How she cried out, begging Shawn to love her, beat her, cherish her, enslave her—anything so long as they might spend the rest of their lives together on this divan in such a manner!

Tania's orgasm was accomplished with complete self-abandon. Shawn, to my surprise, was more controlled. There came a point when she thrust her hips out a little harder and when Tania had to use her tongue more energetically. Then with clenched teeth and a tense, quick palpitation of her brown thighs, our Caribbean beauty also came safe into the calm waters of love's haven.

Following this, they played with one another in the same posture. But there was a sense of calm now, as if they were merely a pair of schoolgirls curiously exploring one another's secret anatomies. This continued for about half an hour, until one sensed that excitement of a more adult kind was beginning to gather once more.

Judi spoke not a word. But, at this point, she returned suddenly through the door and caught the two culprits in the very act. The truth was that, though they must have heard her approach, this pair of lovers was now in a state where neither cared for the world or its reprimands.

"Undress at once!" said Judi sharply, "both of you! Tania has more than convicted herself of wanton behaviour. In your case, Shawn, you have proved yourself a most shameless accomplice!"

Judi stood there, a severe young woman with her short, blond plait, her riding breeches and blouse, the leather switch flexed in the firm grip of her hands.

"Since you are so eager for illicit passion with one another," she went on, "we will make the punishment fit the crime. On this occasion; however, your ecstasies will be tempered by the sharp sauce of chastisement!"

I vow, Charlie, I could scarcely believe my ears! In one afternoon I was to witness things which most men and women might wait a lifetime to see—and would often await in vain! There was no doubt in my mind that the scene about to be played out in that room was to be one of amorous punishment or of disciplined lasciviousness. It was that greatest of love's curiosities which you and I, in our familiar conversation, have often referred to jokingly as "Birch in the Boudoir." And yet, my sweet, often as we have talked about such things, it was not until this afternoon that I began to have some clear conception of the reality.

Alas, it grows late. I must save the remnant of my experiences for tomorrow's letter. You have no idea how the servants talk in such a place as this! Merely for the light to burn in the room of the envoy's daughter until 2 A.M. is sufficient to start all sorts of rumours. You know, my dear, that there can be no ground for them. Others might be less charitable. So I bid you a gentle and loving goodnight until tomorrow, when I will reveal the strange secret which I now share with Nabyla, Judi, Tania, and Shawn!

Your ever-loving Lizzie

Ramallah, 5 May 1904

My dearest Charles,

BEFORE I CONTINUE my account of yesterday's female debaucheries, I must tell you of the great joy I have had in receiving all your dear letters by this morning's post. They came in a single batch, for you know the post is weekly here rather than daily. Oh, how happy I am at the improvement in your prospects by the legacy of your dear Uncle Brandon! How sensibly this must affect dearest Mama and dearest Papa in their estimate of your worthiness as a husband! How strange, my dearest, that families care so greatly for a man's wealth and nothing for his abilities in the bedroom, where a woman's true happiness is made or marred!

I am delighted that your apprenticeship is served in so diverting an establishment as Greystones. What stories we shall have to tell one another by the time we meet again! I am true to my bargain, Charlie. You may indulge in whatever indiscretions you please now, for it will make you a better and a steadier husband if that happy day should ever dawn. What a depraved young slut that Maggie of yours is,

60

however! And how richly you rewarded Maggie and
Noreen in their respective ways. I am surprised that
you have not already whipped Noreen's bottom for
her, as she richly deserves. Perhaps, though, by the
time I have written this letter, you may have reme-
died that omission!

Let me tell you now of my own adventure, or
rather of what passed when Judi returned to Tania
and Shawn yesterday afternoon. Blond and severe in
her riding costume, she flexed the switch between
her hands and watched the two girls undress. She
had, of course, released Tania from the divan, but,
once the undressing was completed, she required
each girl to wear a number of well-polished black
straps. These adorned the waist, the wrists, the neck,
the ankles, and the thighs just above the knees. You
may be sure there was intense nervousness in Tania's
blue eyes at what lay ahead, though Shawn's expression, darkly slanting and tight lidded, was enigmatic.

At first sight you might have thought Judi pro-
posed to roast the two girls on a spit! I hasten to
assure you that such was not the case. Yet she summoned two guards who brought in a strange apparatus, consisting of two supports with a long pole between them. The machinery showed clearly that this
pole could be turned, if so desired, by the person operating it.

Tania and Shawn were attached tightly to the
pole, pressed together and facing one another with
the shaft running between them. Their ankles were
strapped together at one end of it and their wrists at
full stretch above their heads to the far end. The
pole, being metal, was thin though strong, so that
their two bellies almost touched and their breasts
kissed lightly under their own delectable weight. The

two leather neck-collars were attached so that the
girls' lips and tongues were in constant contact.

So these two delicious chickens were hoisted on
their spit about three or four feet above the floor.
Their lips and tongues mingled with promiscuous little moanings of desire. They smoothed their breasts
firmly against one another's until four nipples stood
hard as berries. At one end, the fingers of their
cuffed hands entwined and tightened lovingly. Their
legs and thighs were pressed tight to one another by
the strapping. What a charming picture they made!
Tania, with her cropped brown curls, her pretty little
cherub face, firm, broad hips and muddy-white
skin! Shawn with her Caribbean grace, high-boned
elegance, long legs, and well-curved breasts and buttocks!

The pole turned, just as a roasting spit would. It
might be turned by another person operating its handle, but the controlling wheel could also be urged
forward by vigorous writhing of the girls attached to it.

Judi's face seemed sharp-eyed and expressionless
as she took some hot-spiced paste on her finger,
moistened it with saliva, and spread it on each of the
girls' nipples. The hot irritant drove them into still
more energetic writhing and mutual rubbing. Judi
also smoothed the same erotic heat into each vaginal
slit. Between each girl's legs, she attached to the pole
a convenient dildo so aimed that it would move
within their love-holes by the surging of their hips
but could not be dislodged entirely. Writhing pas-
sionately against one another, each cunt riding its
rubber penis, the two girls faced each other, side by
side or one above the other as their struggling turned
the pole. Tania's mouth swam with Shawn's saliva,
and then as they turned it was Shawn who was
flooded with the tastes of Tania's mouth. With torsos

thrust out, they rubbed their nipples hard against each other. The ingenious dildoes enabled each girl to be simultaneously the lover and mistress of the other.

Was this indeed the punishment they were to suffer? It seemed little enough like punishment to me! But Judi had not quite finished. She took two small rubber cushions, each very firm and about the size of a small plate. Each in turn, she forced one of these under the girls' lions so that their two backsides were thrust out quite hard.

Tania was writhing and squirming at the top of the pole, offering her rear view, while Shawn whimpered amorously from the lower position. Tania's pretty, sun-kissed face, with its clustering brown curls, was hidden as she applied her mouth to Shawn's. Her hips were working hard on the dildo, the cheeks of her bottom alternately arching out and contracting, parting widely and tensing together.

Judi raised the switch and brought it down across the broad weight of Tania's backside. I leave you to imagine the impact of a leather riding switch across Tania's bare arse-cheeks! Her cry was muffled by the pressure of Shawn's lips on her own and the busy wriggling of the Caribbean beauty's tongue in her mouth. Tania's backside squirmed desperately under the lingering smart but even this movement increased the exquisite sensations of the dildo, which was so snugly in her cunt. Judi touched the leather switch lightly upon Tania's bum and gave two more pistol-cracking strokes across the full whiteish cheeks. Even at twenty years old, Tania had never tasted such anguish—nor such pleasure. Had her straps been undone, I wonder if she could have endured to part with the dildo and Shawn's loving even to save her behind from its punishment?

Judi printed a pair of swollen stripes across Tania's bottom-cheeks, enough to drive the girl into turning the pole by her writhing. As she swung into the lower position, sobbing with anguish and desire, so Shawn was turned arse-upwards for Judi's attention.

Imagine the target presented by our Caribbean beauty with her long, graceful brown legs and the dusty gold of her trim but softly luscious seat-cheeks! Even the top-knot of dark hair, with its pretty comb, and the tight-lidded almond eyes seemed to make her a more appealing subject for Judi's vengeance.

Shawn was trying to watch Judi from the corner of her eye. To her dismay, she saw the riding mistress lock the wheel into position so that the pole would not turn.

"Twelve extra strokes before the game begins, Shawn," said Judi quietly, "your punishment for a betrayal of trust. Ah, you can't stop loving yourself on the dildo, can you? Give Tania your tongue properly at the same time—right into her mouth. How hot and swollen your nipples look! Still stinging a little from the spice? Keep rubbing them on Tania's tits, you young bitch."

So saying, Judi measured the riding switch across the dusty-gold cheeks of Shawn's bottom. Once, twice, and again the strokes rang out. The Caribbean girl's seat of beauty was soon striped by several swollen weals. Now the next strokes across Shawn's bottom must fall upon these. The anticipation of doing this was almost too much for Judi to endure. With an impetuosity belying her severity, she undid her riding breeches and laid them down round her knees.

A word of command was given somewhere beyond the latticework on the far side. Into the room came Connie, a beautiful Chinese girl of Judi's own age, naked except for the silver clips holding back the sheen of black hair which fell to her shoulder blades. Obediently, Connie knelt behind her mistress and applied lips and fingers to Judi's venereal anatomy. In this way, she was able to ensure the blond woman's pleasure without interfering in the chastisement. Muffled in her turn by Tania's mouth, Shawn received eight more strokes across her backside, two of them causing wet rubies to glimmer on warm-toned seat-cheeks.

When the wheel was unlocked, the pole turned again under the energetic riding and squirming of Shawn's hips. Tania contrived briefly to free her mouth from Shawn's and turn her face in a wild expression of anguish and ecstasy, pleasure and frenzy. Judi managed to give several strokes across the broad, young cheeks of Tania's bottom before the positions were reversed once more and it was Shawn whose rear-cheeks were turned upwards for discipline.

I swear, Charlie, that, as the performance went on, I do not believe either Shawn or Tania felt anything like the so-called agony of the whipping. It acted merely as a stimulus to desire, in the same manner as the hot irritant paste, which had been applied remorselessly to the most sensitive buds and clefts of their anatomy.

Though Judi, with her severe-looking plait and her keen, blue eyes stood widely astride for Connie's attention, the strictness of her expression never faltered. 'Round and 'round went the spit with the two writhing, hip-pumpiing girls upon it. The leather switch sang out across each bare bottom in turn: Tania's, Shawn's, then Tania's again. The dildo shafts sank and rose again from their furry nests. In the heat of the room, Tania was sweltering. A gloss of perspiration appeared in the small of her back, under her arms, on the inner surfaces of her thighs, and between the cheeks of her bottom. Such energy she was putting into her loving and writhing! For the first time Judi's severe features softened in a smile.

"Your punishment has hardly begun yet, Tania!"

Punishment? It was not the word I would have chosen! Tania's broad, young hips rode up and down, up and down, on the rubber shaft as if her very life depended on it.

I believe that Judi's true excitement came from her sense of power over the two girls. Perhaps she thought of Tania before her abduction into slavery. How many men and women envied those clustering curls, the pretty dimpling of her face? How many were haunted by a glimpse of Tania bending, chin in hands, as she read a book, offering such a provokingly full rear view?

Judi locked the wheel into place as Tania lay arse-upwards.

"Twelve strokes for your wantonness, Tania!"

The blond mistress kept her waiting for several minutes. Even during this time, Tania never ceased to ride the dildo or to fill Shawn's mouth with her tonguing and kissing.

At last it came, an amorous whipping whose agonising strokes served only to drive the "victim" into further and more desperate loving. However bruised or swollen Tania's bottom might be, however appalling the menace of further strokes, it was only what Judi called it: the sharp sauce of a greater pleasure.

You may imagine, Charlie, that I sat there immobile and watched until Judi sank to her knees, conquered by Connie's busy tongue. The fulfilment of the mistress brought respite at last to the two miscreants.

It seemed that the curtain was about to be rung down on this first scene of a harem "comedy." Yet Nabyla had been sent on an errand and I was compelled to wait for her return before leaving my place. That being so, I was privileged not only to see the drama itself but also the epilogue.

Tania and Shawn were released. They left with their arms about one another, cooing or sobbing gently together like a pair of doves. Each bottom, Tania's broad and pale, Shawn's taut and brown, bore the prints of the leather switch. Judi followed them to the bedroom, where the three would pass a night of passion together.

What of poor Connie, I wondered? She dressed herself in a pair of tight, denim knickers from waist to knee—such as Tania wore—and a short, blue tunic ening at her waist. Her task was to put the room to rights. Sitting on her heels, she began to collect the debris from the floor. What a charming picture she made! Connie's rather flat features and slanting eyes are set in a face of heart-shaped delicacy. Like so many girls of her Asiatic beauty, she can assume a beautiful impassivity or a devil mask of laughter with equal ease. Her figure, like her face, has a slim, fine-boned appearance.

As Connie worked, I saw a tall, fair-whiskered English Milord of twenty-five pass the open door. I imagined him to be one of the Pasha's privileged guests. He stopped and surveyed Connie from her slim thighs and tautly rounded bum-cheeks to her slim shoulders, on which the black hair with its silver clips fell in a fine curtain. He watched her from this way and that, as if photographing upon his mind the images of her kneeling, stretching, bending. It was some time before Connie realised that she was under observation. When she did so, there was nothing for it but to continue her work while shooting a glance of sudden apprehension at the man from time to time. Presently he went away. Later he came back. I can scarcely describe the sudden shock in Connie's eyes when she saw him standing there once more, watching her. But this time he entered the spacious, well-appointed room, closing the door after him, and locking it.

"Your master has given you to me for a night of pleasure, Connie," he said, sitting on the divan. "Come to me naked and kneel down before me."

I truly believe that Nabyla left me there deliberately to witness what followed. Connie's knickers came down and her tunic off. This demure, submissive Asian beauty then knelt before her English lover. Without a word of command, she undid his trousers with her slim, quick fingers and drew out his penis. She touched her lips to it, ran her tongue 'round its knob, and, as it stiffened, took it in her mouth. The curtains of her black hair covered his thighs as she sucked. He made her suck for five or ten minutes, then restrained her briefly, then motioned her to start again.

Later she climbed meekly onto the divan, lay on her back with legs apart and feet raised, guiding him down and sheathing his quivering dart between her thighs. As he rode her, she softly taught him how to nip her with his teeth, to flick her breast buds with his tongue, to rake her flanks with his nails in the fury of desire. Later still, she turned over on her belly, offering the rear view of her trim, saffron-yellow figure, with the black, silken hair spread on the shoulder blades. Connie's bottom had those pale-yellow cheeks which are soft but neatly rounded. She had obviously been well trained in a slave girl's submission, for no word of command was needed even now. She reached back and pulled her buttocks apart, hiding her face bashfully in the pillow as she offered the tight dimple of her anus to the man's lust. He buggered Connie with such energy that she several times drew a sharp breath. He spent in her neat, young Chinese bottom and she thanked him charmingly.

Then she looked at him with great apprehension. She slid from the divan, walked across to the cupboard with a delicious little swagger of her bare hips, and produced a birch. Its three, yard-long switches were bound at the handle in the way that prison rods are. With eyes lowered, she took it back to him, presented it to him kneeling, and then bent herself forward over the back of a chair.

I could not guess what his response would be, for his tool now hung remarkably slack. First, he secured her wrists to the wooden legs. Then he took his place behind her and touched the long birch switches to the broad, well-separated cheeks of Connie's trim backside.

"If I were a judge, condemning you as a thieving shopgirl, Connie," he said coolly, "I should order you eighteen strokes of the prison birch. I must not be too timid to carry out such acts for myself."

The birch made a soft, lashing sound as it cut across the pale-yellow cheeks of Connie's bottom, its fine tips curling 'round to catch her flanks. Even now there was a softness in her cries, as if she knew that a respite was impossible and that to scream for it would be a sign of defiance. The familiar raised scratches of the birching, long and curling, soon traversed her buttocks. Two or three times the birch just missed its target and caught her high on the legs. When it was over, her lover set her free, and led her back to the divan.

Now Connie had her reward. He placed her gently on her back and rode into her cunt with renewed lust so searchingly that Connie cried out with a greater intensity of joy than when she cried in distress during her tanning. They fell asleep together after the climax like a devoted bride and groom.

At two in the morning, her lover woke her gently, stroking her face. He required his Asian bride-of-a-night to turn onto her belly. He then made love to Connie's bottom. Little more than an hour passed before he woke her once more, this time spreading her legs and taking his way between them. In the pale, star-lit flush preceding dawn, their sleep was broken once more.

"Your bottom again, Connie," he murmured, as she stirred under his caresses. "Hold the cheeks well apart and rest your belly on the pillow. Arch your rump out even farther. . . ."

I can scarcely describe the many sequels, as I am exhausted by my vigil. You may protest at a young lady writing of such things, but it is the very truth, as witnessed by

Your own adoring Lizzie

Darling Lizzie,

*W*ITH WHAT relief did I receive your letters at last and learn that all is well with you at Ramallah! You may be sure that I read with great amusement the frisky doings of Tania and Shawn, as well as the amorous ordeal of Connie! I fear, my sweet, that you may find the news of Greystones dull by contrast, for there is much to be done in a harem which would be imprudent here!

Nonetheless, these past few days have produced one or two diverting little incidents among the stable-girls who are my chief concern even now. It is almost as if Miss Martinet believes I may find greater pleasure in their randy company than among the refined young ladies of fourteen in her sewing class. Who can say but that she may be right?

Since I last wrote to you, two more young women have come under my care, though they are ten years different in age. Jacqueline, the elder, is truly a self-regarding slut of twenty-five. She pretends to education and refinement but is, I feel sure, a young trollop who cannot get her pants off fast enough if it suits her purpose! She is not quite in her first youth, though she presents a challenge to any man. Her straight, blond hair has been cut in a short bell shape with a fringe, the style of the reformatory from which she came. Such dismissive blue eyes, Lizzie, so pert a nose and such heavy sulkiness in the mouth and jaw! In singlet and working trousers, her figure is not overblown, though I wager she may run to fat in a few years more—certainly if her belly swells with a brat! Her breasts are bouncy, her legs quite long and still trim. If you see her in tight, working trousers from the front there is an outward curve of her belly which suggests she may already have dropped a brat on the sly! On the inner edge of her thighs, either side of her cunt, a fleshy bulge swells out the cloth. Tell me, Lizzie, is this not one of the first signs of fat? If you see her turn and bend in fawn riding tights, Jackie's bottom is seductively fattish but not yet too much so for me. Under her disdainful manner, however, she is extremely wanton and eager.

My younger charge, Amanda Ticklepuss, known as Mandy, is fifteen years old. Yet she is quite tall and strongly built, with long, firm legs and sturdy hips which give her quite a broad and Amazonian arse. True to type, Mandy has a strong-featured face, softened by a pleasant, smiling manner and gentle waves of chestnut hair, which are combed loose to her shoulders—such a beautiful reddish tint.

After the randiness of many of the young bitches at Greystones, I was quite taken aback by Jackie's display of disdain and her pretence of injured virtue whenever one tipped her breast, stroked her thighs, or pinched her arse-cheeks lightly. I was almost deceived by this. Then, one morning, I was invited to attend Miss Martinet in order to discuss some manner of business. Silas Raven, the surly old brief, was coming down to Greystones—at our expense—to discuss some matter connected with my Uncle Brandon's will. I informed the grooms that I should not be visiting the stables that day, for I envisaged a prime lunch and a good blow-out.

As I waited with Miss M., a telegram arrived. There had been a most unfortunate incident in the gentlemen's lavatory at Victoria Station. The door of one of the cubicles had become wedged and two uniformed police constables had been summoned in the general alarm. When the door was freed by these two stalwarts, out tumbled Silas Raven and two young guardsmen in *déshabillé*. The young soldiers were all for laying the constabulary senseless and making off. Silas Raven prevented the necessity. A few moments later, the entire party went its separate ways, the pockets of the two policemen chinking with sovereigns, and the zealous officers of the law saluting S. Raven, Esquire, as if he might be the Prince of Wales and Lord Rosebery all in one.

Yet after so disturbing an entree to the railway station, the respected counsel from Grays Inn was far too shaken to contemplate a journey that day. In consequence, Miss M. and I found ourselves at what is colloquially termed "a loose end."

It was a fine summer morning, the chestnut candles still upon the trees, and I thought it no hardship to stroll back to the stables and perhaps from there to the cliff walk and the sea. I made no great sign of my approach, walking slowly and in some depth of thought. Only as I approached did I realise that some kind of revelry was taking place in the stable block. This gave me pause. By good fortune, there was a side door which led directly into my own little office. The wall between the office and the main sta-

ble boasted one of those miniature internal windows
which save folk the necessity of walking all the way
'round to the door when some paper or small object
is to be handed through. Unobserved, I might yet
discover the nature of the stable celebration.

I slipped in quietly and went across to the little
window. Sure enough I had a fine view of all that
was passing in my absence—or so everyone there believed. Jackie and Mandy were at the centre of the
excitement, the two grooms were at one end of the
room, and the stable boys at the other.

Twenty-five-year-old Jackie did not look as if she
had been a volunteer for these japes. Under the bell
shape of blond hair, her mouth was hard and sullen,
her blue eyes frostily dismissive. She was twisting in
the arms of the two men who held her, for they were
trying to get her pants off.

The singlet parted company from her pants at the
waist. She wriggled 'round. Now they had her bending, the tight, fawn riding trousers showing me her
long, firm legs and the fattish cheeks of her arse as
she stooped.

Fortunately the grooms soon undid the belt and
pushed Jackie's pants down to her ankles. They
threw her on the pile of straw, where she lay on her
belly looking up at them over her shoulder. There
was still hostility in her blue eyes as she shook the
hair into place after the struggle. Her long legs were
pressed tightly together as she lay there and the pale,
fattish cheeks of her bottom were similarly tensed.
  The first groom stood over her, muscular legs
astride and the crotch of his tight breeches now swollen with the size of his erection. He unbuttoned himself and released the stout weapon. The sluttish
young blonde defied him, continuing to lie face-
down. Slowly, the groom drew the broad leather belt

from his waist. Holding the two ends, he placed a foot gently on the young woman's neck to hold her, and brought down the strap half a dozen times across the white quivering cheeks of Jackie's broad, young arse.

With a cry she obeyed him as soon as her neck was released, turning on to her back, knees hugged up, and thighs open. He knelt at her, adjusting his penis to her love-hole.

"You'll enjoy it more for having had your arse strapped, Jackie!" he said humorously. Then he pressed home.

How Jackie loved it! Such sighs and soft crying, as her heels touched the small of her lover's back! When the penis accidentally slipped out of her cunt, she gave such a doleful cry at the loss of its comfort—and such a sob of contentment when it was replaced.

The groom pulled up the front of the blond girl's singlet and busied his mouth with her breasts. He kissed and flicked the nipples with his tongue. Then he gently and lovingly bit her shoulders and her neck. Jackie's own crisis came before his, in a series of short, rising cries. Yet the excitement of her fulfilment soon precipitated his own warm flooding of her cunt. The second groom ordered the young blonde to kneel on all fours, as he released his splendid tool from his pants.

What a sight was this! Our impudent young blonde now knelt like a bitch waiting to be mounted—and mounted she soon was! The second groom rode into her cunt with even more vigour than the first. Yet in his hand he also held a blob of saddle soap, well moistened by his saliva. Presently he used this to prepare the tight bud of Jackie's anus. Drawing from her cunt, he thrust hard and impaled her twenty-five-year-old bottom in the style of a champion. The young woman gave a cry of surprise rather than discomfort. Yet he entered so easily that I feel sure Jackie had been up to this sort of mischief with other men. She loves the penis, cannot get enough of it, and will take it in any way rather than be without it.

"You'll be getting a nice thick pressing of juice up your arse, Jackie!" gasped the groom. "Lie still now and enjoy it!"

His words were proved right almost at once. Yet, while he was busy with the young blonde, the first groom had gone over to the stable-lads, who held Mandy between them. Perhaps she was not a girl to struggle with, for at fifteen years old she was tall, long-legged, and strongly made. The firmness of her pale features and chin was softened by the chestnut-red of the hair which was combed in gentle waves to her shoulders.

The stable-lads were rather young for the antics of the grooms with Jackie and none of them could rival Mandy's fifteen years. Yet they had a natural curiosity and excitement about the way in which little girls—and big girls too—were made. Mandy's long legs and sturdy hips were tightly encased in riding jeans, which the groom now ordered her to take off. She looked at him with uncertain defiance.

"Want the strap across your bottom, Mandy?" he asked, "like Jackie had it! No? Take them off, then!"

Imagine, as she obeyed, how the lads clustered 'round! Some stroked her long, firm thighs, others were bold enough to fiddle with her love-pouch, a few preferred to slip their fingers between the strong, young cheeks of Mandy's arse.

"Lie over the pile of straw, Mandy!" said the

groom. "Pull your singlet right up and show us those luscious young breasts!"

So our long-legged maiden tugged the singlet up under her armpits and lay back on the straw, looking up at the stable-lads with quiet amusement as they goggled at her.

"Want to be a dirty girl, Mandy?" said the groom, smiling at her. Mandy grinned back, as if they shared some secret, her strong chin and steady eyes challenging him. "Do it lying over the straw, Mandy!" he chuckled, handing her something closed in his fist.

It was Mandy's party trick, greatly admired by the lads. She took from the groom two china pullet eggs, each the size of a large plum. She popped them into her mouth and made a swallowing movement twice.

"Jackie!" called the groom, now that his colleague had finished with that luscious young blonde, "over here! Play at dirty girls with Mandy on the straw!"

Jackie obeyed, and we enjoyed the sight of the strapping, young Amazon of fifteen and the fat-arsed blonde of twenty-five writhing naked in each other's arms. Presently, Mandy sat up, with a look of feigned dismay. She parted her bare thighs and looked as the two pullet eggs popped out of her cunt! Her open mouth showed they truly had gone! The grooms turned, presenting the rear of her long legs, strong hips, her strapping young arse, and the auburn hair on her bare shoulders. The two china ovals were popped into Mandy's arse-hole. More writhing in Jackie's arms and then another look of dismay. Opening her lips like a magician, Mandy showed the little white eggs in her mouth once more.

It was easy, of course, but effective and rather charming. The stable-lads cheered and guffawed.

Clearly there were several pairs of china eggs.
Mandy transferred the two from her mouth into
Jackie's as they kissed, then produced the two which
had been lodged in her cunt before the show had begun. As they were thumbed into Mandy's arse, she
took the first pair back from Jackie's mouth. Now
Jackie's bottom produced another pair from between
its fattish cheeks.

I was most diverted by the antics of the stable-
lads—the manner in which these amiable young
scamps amused themselves with Mandy and Jackie!
Yet prudence dictated that I should not reveal my
presence just then. I slipped out of the side door and
crossed the sunlit lawns towards the main house.
Perhaps I might entertain Miss Martinet at luncheon
with stories of my past adventures.

Just then my attention was caught by the sight of
one of Miss M.'s well-bred young pupils making her
way to the music room. Vanessa was just short of
her fifteenth birthday and in every way a contrast to
a plump-bottomed slut like Jackie or even a strapping young wench of Mandy's type. Because she is
rather short, Vanessa looks perter than her years.
She was dressed just then in her white blouse and
striped tie, the dark-blue skirt, which came down to
the middle of her calves, and a pair of white ankle
socks. Is she seductive? Who can say? Her brown
hair is cut straight, in a casque shape which ends at
her collar, her fringe parted on her forehead. Vanessa has a lightly sun-browned face, prettily heart-
shaped with high cheekbones and light-blue eyes that
have a narrow, crinkling mockery in them. She has
the firm, clear-cut nose and chin of the well-bred
high-school girl.

There is still a childish slovenliness about her
which, in a grown woman, would be sluttish. The

movements of her hips and thighs have a slow heaviness which lacks mature feminine grace. Left to herself, she would no doubt have grown up as a very self-centred young lady. How fortunate that she could be brought under discipline at Greystones. If Vanessa is to be chastised in any case, it may as well be by those who enjoy it!

I watched her enter the music room and I spied through the large picture window to see what she would do. To my surprise, Miss Martinet was already in there. I could not hear what passed between them, but the dumb-show itself was most eloquent.

Miss M. unbuttoned Vanessa's blouse and untied the school tie, baring the young pupil above her waist except for her breast halter. Her skirt was next removed. Vanessa's calves and thighs lack a mature woman's shape as yet, being midway between the lumpishness of an adolescent child and the grace of a young nymph. She now wore her white ankle socks and a pair of tight, stretched briefs made of white cotton web, the first sign that she was due for a dancing lesson.

Miss Martinet stood close, kissed Vanessa lightly on the lips, and began to work the briefs down over the youngster's hips and thighs. I stared with fascination, wondering if fourteen-year-old Vanessa would be compelled to have Lesbian sex with her mistress. Miss M. led her to a chair and sat down. She put Vanessa over her knee and stroked the bare back and hips for a moment. The taut, adolescent pallor of Vanessa's bottom-cheeks was so prominently presented that I thought she was due for a spanking from Miss Martinet, but that was not what happened.

The mistress slid a hand through the rear opening of the schoolgirl's thighs and began to fondle Vanessa's vaginal pouch and clitoris. The pupil gasped and squirmed with the excitement of this delicious masturbation. She did not climax, but the lubrication began to flow in her young cunt and soon one could see its slipperiness on her inner thighs as well as on her love-purse itself.

What do you imagine Miss M. did next? She took some discs of red sticky paper, each the size of a small coin. One by one she wetted them with Vanessa's cunt juice and then stuck them here and there on the woman-child's body. The breast halter was removed and they were pasted to her blossoming tits. They were stuck to her belly, her thighs, and between her thighs. Yet more were glued lightly to Vanessa's taut, pale bottom-cheeks and some on her fourteen-year-old arse-hole. Then she was made to stand up.

Can you guess what was about to happen, Lizzie! I vow I could not. Never fear, my sweet. The mystery shall be revealed in tomorrow night's letter from your own adoring,

Charles

Greystones, 3 June 1904

My darling Lizzie,

I NOW RESUME my account of the other day's adventures. Picture Vanessa, naked but for her white ankle socks, standing at the centre of the polished boards which form the floor of the music room. Her wrists are strapped together in front of her. A leather collar 'round her neck is attached to a slack cord which hangs from the beam above her, thus keeping her in one area of the floor.

I could not hear whether there was the music of tambourine and flute, yet Vanessa now began the sinuous writhing of a harem dance. So clumsy she seemed for fourteen, though there was a knowingness in that light, olive-skinned face, with its mocking blue eyes and well-cut features, under the fringe of her casque of brown hair.

She knelt open-legged before her mistress's chair and began to shake her pert young breasts eagerly. I could see Miss M.'s lips forming her words slowly.

"Have you been fondling and playing with your tits as I ordered, Vanessa, to fill them out? Good.

Come to my room each evening at nine and show me how you do it."

The aim of the dance was to shake free the tiny discs of paper stuck to the youngster's body. At last they began to spiral like autumn leaves from Vanessa's sweet little breasts. Miss Martinet leant forward, took each nipple in turn, and erected it firmly with her skillful tongue. Vanessa rose and began arching and rolling her taut belly at Miss M., offering it to her kisses. By this means she contrived to make the mistress's lips brush her flat and taut abdomen, thus freeing more of the paper discs. Then, leaning far back, the pupil offered her splayed thighs, writhing them seductively to dislodge the red circles pasted between. Miss M.'s finger caressed Vanessa's love-slit until the schoolgirl thighs trembled from quite a different cause.

By squirming her thighs together, Vanessa managed to dislodge most of the discs on their inner surfaces, but those on her cunt itself proved so tenacious. Smiling, Miss Martinet intruded her fingers between Vanessa's squirming adolescent thighs so that her dancing pupil might smooth herself upon them and so free the little paper discs which clung there. With how many soft schoolgirl sighs and gasps were they dislodged!

Her mistress took a towel and rubbed it lightly between the girl's thighs, squeezing Vanessa's love-purse dry in such a manner as to bring her close to orgasm. Now the petite high-school charmer turned. The cheeks of Vanessa's bottom had the pale taut-ness and elasticity of childhood but also the first traces of a woman's more voluptuous fullness. She leant forward a little and writhed her seat-cheeks at Miss Martinet, as if trying to seduce the older woman by this performance.

Miss Martinet was not smiling now. She craned forward a little, lips pressed hard. Vanessa's arse-cheeks surged and parted so innocently. Miss Martinet chose a tawse, a broad lightweight strap, divided into three tails at its end. Vanessa's backside did a desperate jungle dance, but the obstinate red discs of paper still clung.

The mistress used the strap across the bare writhing cheeks of Vanessa's bottom. She caught the youngster on the backs of the thighs as well. Six times the leather exploded on the cheeks of Vanessa's fourteen-year-old backside. Twice more on her thighs. She tried to turn 'round, to shield her buttocks, but the strap kissed her flank savagely.

As the last paper disc fluttered down, Vanessa sank to the floor exhausted. Miss Martinet ceased to be the tyrant and became the lover once more. She knelt beside Vanessa, gently stroking the casque of brown hair, comforting and caressing until her fingers slipped at last between the rather ungainly adolescent thighs. Vanessa's sobs became soft, questioning sighs of wonder. Miss Martinet kissed the tears from the eyes of her high-school pupil. With gentle skill, she brought Vanessa to a crescendo for ten or fifteen minutes.

Then I saw a curious thing: to one side of the room was a long curtain, reaching from the ceiling to within an inch or two of the floor. From under the curtain protruded a foot in a black, patent-leather shoe. In front of the concealed figure, whose excitement seemed to come from watching Vanessa, there knelt a young woman whose name was spoken as Julie. I recognised this as belonging to a nineteen-year-old girl in Miss Martinet's possession. Julie was one of those slender young women who make up their height by high heels, and whose thighs are no thicker than a man's upper arm.

Julie is a slut as surely as any girl in the establishment. Through a chink in the curtain I could make out her sulky, sour little face with its rather crude features and dark, hazel eyes. Her blond hair had been braided into a plait and was pinned up in a top-knot, revealing her slender little neck. I can imagine how the men who were served by her in the shop where she worked must have coveted her. What would they have said now to see Julie rhythmically and expertly sucking the penis?

As she knelt at her task, her thighs were so slender, and yet the slight backward jut of her hips gave a certain rather childish fatness to the shape of her bottom-cheeks. There was a senile crowing from her lover and Julie was obliged to swallow down her repugnance. Two veined and gnarled old hands held her head close while the old man's sperm-spasm loaded her tongue and he made her gulp it down.

I walked slowly to the front entrance of the house, wondering who the old leacher might be. There, outside the handsome portico, I saw the private carriage of Silas Raven, K.C., in all the majesty of the law.

They had not seen me, of course, and yet I could not bring myself to go in and face the pair at luncheon. Instead, I took a stroll in the pleasant summer gardens above the sea for an hour and then resolved, since the pranks in the stable must be over, to return to my office there.

As I had surmised, the stable was silent and deserted. I wondered where the two grooms might be, and whether they had taken Jackie and Maggie with them. It seemed a day of midsummer madness, when lechery was enthroned in men's minds—and women's too! I remembered that there was a hundred-yard length of chain, stretching down the cliff to a buoy in the shallows, which had to be wound onto the spool of the old mill wheel. The grooms had been told by Miss M. to see it done that afternoon. I went down almost as far as the old miller's grinding wheel, unused for many a day, and stopped short. Nothing I had seen so far on this midsummer day equalled the present spectacle.

The grooms had devised an ingenious scheme for drawing the long chain up the cliff and 'round the grinding wheel, to which one end was already attached. The wheel had a yoke across it, protruding at either side, to which beasts of burden had once been attached. Some means must be found to turn it now, in a heavy two-hour labour. What ingenious fellows they were!

The blond bell shape of Jackie's hair was clearly seen threshing to and fro as she struggled in their grip. But they bent her forward, leather wrist cuffs and collar holding her down on the yoke bar on one side of the wheel. Once she was bent over so tightly and helplessly, they fondled the fattened seat of her bronze-toned riding jeans only briefly before taking those pants right off her and baring her below the waist.

To ensure her arousal, they tightened a strap 'round each of Jackie's thighs and attached to it an ingenious love feather pointing upwards on the inside of her thigh. With every step she took, the tantalising feathers would tickle her cunt, masturbating blond, twenty-five-year-old Jackie irresistibly.

To ensure this, the grooms now massaged Jackie's vaginal slit with warm irritant spice powder. Every teasing tickle of the feathers would be a piercing thrill to her inflamed and itching cunt-pouch. Imagine Jackie, bending with wrists and neck strapped to the yoke bar. Her pale legs are quite long and trim, her bottom rather fatly cheeked in this pose, the tingling cunt-lips clearly visible between her thighs. Jackie's plump, young tits were still quite firm, but as they hung down now they jigged a little as she squirmed. Ah, the young scamp with the spice licked his fingers, dipped them in, and rubbed the virulent itch powder into Jackie's nipples. What a change came over that sullen young face, its blue eyes, hard jaw, and mouth under the fringe of her blond bell shape of hair! Jackie, so off-hand and indifferent in serving men, now cried out to have her tits rubbed and sucked, and the fiery itching soothed by any means her lovers chose!

I was delighted to see that they were still not quite satisfied with her predicament. The groom took a false pony-tail of hair, which matched Jackie's own blond colour. Its base was a leather butt, two inches long, and thick as a thumb. Grinning at the young blonde, he showed her a jar of vaseline, took a blob on his finger, and smeared it thickly on Jackie's arsehole! Even so, she gave a gasp as he forced the butt into her anus. The tail was drawn up her buttock-crack, under her belt, and then arched in a charming curve, its ends just sweeping the top of her buttocks.

Fifteen-year-old Mandy was strapped bending to the yoke bar on the other side in the same way. Whenever she bent over, the tight seat of Mandy's jeans shows a strapping young backside, broad-cheeked and strongly made, without yet being spoilt by flabbiness. They took her pants down, strapped the masturbation feathers to her long firm thighs, and rubbed her cunt and nipples with the stinging spice. The artificial pony-tail matched those lightly waving chestnut tresses, which softened the firm lines of Mandy's young face and caught the colour of her brown eyes.

They vaselined the tight inward dimple of Mandy's arse-hole and the leather butt was firmly inserted. Mandy, at fifteen years old, may still have been a virgin in that place. Indeed, she cried out. Yet she was so sturdy in that area that one could not expect two high-spirited grooms to abandon their sport for such a quibble.

The grooms can be rascals, of course, but only in a softly suggestive way. The harnessing apparatus included a thin bridle strap between each girl's teeth, which could not be detached from the rest. To prevent chafing, it was necessary to pad the thin leather. Nothing was available for this but the two pairs of knickers discarded on the turf. They could not resist a lewd exchange, padding Jackie's mouth with Mandy's knickers, while Mandy's mouth was protected by the panties still warm from Jackie's bottom and hips.

All was ready for the two hours' labour by this pair of intriguing pony-girls. Harnessed bending to the yoke, they must turn the heavy wheel and draw up the long chain. Jackie shook her bell of blond hair and looked 'round with sullen jaw and insolent blue eyes. Yet she is randy by nature, much more so with the hot spice and feathers which made her cunt-pouch itch and tingle. Now she looked back in a manner of sluttish defiance, deliberately refusing to move. When you know Jackie better, you will realise that the refusal was a pretence. She was almost drunk with lewdness, if a young woman can be. In this sexual intoxication she wanted to provoke the groom to treat her with a lover's discipline.

You do not believe me? I saw Jackie with her foot

slyly edge a loose brick so that it fell into the wheel mechanism. Until it was noticed and removed, the wheel would not turn and she, of course, could utter no words of explanation. The groom brought his hand down hard and stinging, spanking the fatly pale curve of her bottom-cheeks. At last his colleague saw the brick and removed it.

Now Jackie's long thighs shimmered, her hips laboured, and her fattened shopgirl bottom-cheeks arched and contorted as she strained forward. With every arduous step, the quivering feathers tickled an itching cunt. In no time, Jackie's love-slit was weeping pearly droplets of excitement.

Sometimes her need for love was so strong that she stopped, knees buckling and thighs squeezing. Mandy's own situation was no better. All disobedience was now curbed. During Jackie's defiance the second groom had touched his gasper to the cleavage of Mandy's strapping, fifteen-year-old bottom. Now, as she laboured forward with long, lightly muscled legs, Mandy masturbated herself perforce on the cunning feathers.

In the warm afternoon, the two labouring girl-ponies began to perspire a little. Their cunts gave off a delicate mineral scent of feminine arousal. Very soon a faint, musty girl-scent also came from between the cheeks of Jackie's bottom.
Mandy's perspiration between her arse-halves soon contributed to this.

Horse flies and mosquitoes sang eagerly around these savoury areas. The happy insects landed and fed, several at a time, in such veritable clusters. It was true that Jackie and Mandy had pony-tails attached to them, but these merely brushed to and fro across the very tops of their arses, leaving much of their buttocks and thighs without such a fly whisk.

To assist the girls in their plight, each groom armed himself with a broad, thin strap, divided into three tails at its end—the tawse which Miss M. had used upon Vanessa. The two men set up in competition to see which could swat the greater number of flies on the legs and bottom of the girl he attended. The first groom swung his strap with ringing smacks across the pale, fattened cheeks of Jackie's bottom and her thighs. The red spank marks soon blossomed from her waist to her knees. Jackie's arse was spangled with the remains of insects flattened by these blows.

Mandy was more agile and twisted more violently. The tawse sometimes caught her flanks in consequence. Yet Mandy's bottom and thighs received their fair share of a severe strapping. Like Jackie, she was riven by the exquisite thrills between her legs and the smarting ordeal of the strap.

The grooms made the two young women stop for a moment. They now moistened the two love-purses with a thin coat of honey. How intriguing this was. Next the men took two small boxes, each containing a colony of saucy ants, and applied them to these parts of the girls' anatomies!

Can you guess the sequel? The ants began to sting lightly the cunt-lips and bottom cleavages of Jackie and Mandy. It was no punishment, merely the injection of the irritant acid into those most erotically sensitive crevices. The virulence of the itch and the swelling heat, the need for fondling and handling, turned Jackie and Mandy almost demented. All labour ceased. Each of them lay bottom-upwards over her yoke bar, squeezing her thighs hard and rhythmically on her love-slit, whimpering for the hand and penis of her groom.

You may be sure they would soon get their hearts'

desire. Yet first there was a good deal of play about their disobedience. The first groom took his cane. Twenty or thirty whip strokes across the pale, fattish cheeks of Jackie's bottom, which the young blonde did not mind greatly, for it was the spur to her Venus-gallop. The second groom grinned at Mandy as she bent squirming piteously with longing over the bar. The firm young face, with its auburn waves to her bare shoulders, was pleading with desire. He gazed at her strong, broadened young hips, long sturdy legs, and Mandy's strapping, fifteen-year-old arse-cheeks.

Mandy had never had the cane before and she cried out under the first few strokes across her backside. Then her protests also sank to soft questioning whimpers of wanting and needing.

The two hours' labour became four hours . . . six. . . . eight. . . . Darkness fell over that remote part of the grounds. Quiet voices carried in the warm night air.

"Your cunt is so velvet-smooth, Jackie! Yet a swollen belly will make you run to fat, will it not? I shall withdraw. Turn over. Ah, you like the feel of the sperm coming in your bottom, Jackie, you randy young thing! . . . Lie back with legs open and make love to yourself, Mandy. Let me shine the light on you. Now thread yourself on my stiffness. How greatly you enjoy it, Mandy, even though Miss Martinet will cane your backside tomorrow for so long an absence. Does that add to your thrill, Mandy? . . ."

Such, Lizzie, are the sweet words which the summer night carries to

Your own adoring Charlie

NaN*Ramallah, 12 July 1904*

My dearest Charlie,

I HOPE YOU will not be vexed, my precious, at what I have done. Never before, upon my maiden honour, have I shown one of your sweet letters to another living soul. Nor would I have done so now had I not been so intrigued by the manner in which Jackie and Mandy were set to work as "girl-ponies" at Greystones! Such a charming image was conjured up in my mind by your account that I could scarcely rid myself of it.

I know you will forgive me for showing that portion of your letter to our generous Pasha of Ramallah. As you shall hear, my action provoked the most amusing results.

To my surprise, he knew all about such games. Indeed, he said, the sultans and pashas of the East had long been accustomed to employ some of their favourite concubines between the shafts of their little garden carriages. He cited so many instances in history, from Sultan Ibrahim of the Sublime Porte to Mulay Ishmael himself, that I could scarcely hold any further doubts in the matter.

91

"Not twenty miles from here lives Pasha Ibrahim," said he, "a wealthy patriarch of sixty summers. His harem is extensive and, like myself, he is a great lover of English and European beauty. The use of harness, as he calls it, is indispensable to the management of his girls, especially if one of them should prove difficult."

I listened agog, Charlie, for, though I could imagine that such things might happen behind harem walls, it was astonishing to be conforted so quickly with the proof of it.

"Then, sir," I said, "I suppose a great deal of privacy must surround these occasions. The good Pasha Ibrahim would guard such a secret closely."

The Pasha of Ramallah laughed. "Dear young lady! Why do you say so? All the world knows of the means he employs. In this country we think better of a man who is prepared to resort to such measures, provided he thinks them desirable. My brother Ibrahim opens his gardens on such an occasion to his intimate friends, just as he does on other days of hospitality."

Now, Charlie, you may be sure that I questioned our friend so long and so ingeniously about Ibrahim's pony-girls that he soon saw my intention.

"I believe, dear young lady, that you would be ever grateful to me if I could contrive your presence at one of these afternoon outings. Am I not right?"

He was so amused at finding me out, as he thought, that I could only confirm his suspicion as demurely as I knew how. Pray, give me credit, Charlie. You will remember well how I can counterfeit the faint maiden blush, the modest lowering of the gaze, the cloistered innocence of virtue upon these occasions.

"Very well," he said, "nothing could be easier

than for you to accompany me in a day or two on my visit to the happy fellow. I happen to know that he has lately acquired a most rebellious young lass of fifteen, who is more than due for a lesson in obedience."

I need not say how I looked forward with the greatest curiosity to the day of that visit. It seemed best to say nothing of it to my dearest papa and mama, beyond telling them that I was to take tea with Ibrahim's ladies.

It was still morning when we arrived at Ibrahim's estate. Like our friend's, it is set in a green jewel of an oasis, remote from the city, its high surrounding walls well guarded to exclude intruders and immure the occupants. From the carriage window, as we passed along the drive, I was able to glimpse the ornamental pleasure gardens with their winding paths. A fine lake lay at the centre, quite half a mile long. Upon its shore stood replicas of small, pillared temples here and there, such as might have been built for Apollo or Jove, in the ancient world. Banks of mauve, silken-coloured flowers rose on either side, others rising flame-red or fierce blue in the brilliant sun. Elsewhere the trees provided deep, shady retreats where marble fountains played.

Of the house itself I will say only that I was a perfect Alhambra of Moorish courtyards and colonnades, with dazzling sun on the marble and water, restful darkness in the tapestried rooms.

The tyrant Ibrahim, as I had imagined him, was a jovial gentleman with a twinkle in his eye. When the formal courtesies were over, he escorted us to a grassy knoll overlooking his splendid grounds. Here an excellent lunch was served: the most succulent fruits, the crispest roast, and the most savoury dishes were moistened by fine vintages and champagne.

Ibrahim's religion forbid him the use of wine, yet he is too generous a man ever to stint his guests.

It was here that I again saw Connie, the young woman of some twenty-five years, with her Asian or Chinese appearance. The black, silken sweep of her hair was once again held in place by a pair of silver slides so that it did not fall too far over her face. She was not entirely naked, though very nearly so: a pair of tiny cones, made of tight, black silk, covered her nipples, and were held in place by black silk cord over her two shoulders and 'round her back. Her other garment was a black silk cache-sex, a tiny triangle at her loins, held by black cord 'round her waist, its supports running down her belly to the silk adornment, and at the rear running back up to her waist between the cheeks of her bottom.

Several different girls acted as waitresses, Connie being given orders to minister to half a dozen of us. The rather snub features, slanted eyes, and pretty heart-shaped face she has are so very appealing! And what of her figure? No part of the world, I vow, can rival the Far East in that neat feminine charm; the slim, nimble forms, the tight rounds of buttocks, which never grow too fat even in a girl whose hips are broadened by her posture.

As she walked to and fro, the eyes of the men followed the light, graceful movements of her body. They contemplated her pale-yellow satiny skin, her tight little breasts, narrow thighs, and saffron bottom-cheeks. Even when she was on full view as a shopgirl, I cannot believe she received as much admiration in six months as she now got in half an hour.

The meal ended. Now the men lit their cheroots and began to chaff one another. There was much daring of each fellow in turn to grasp a nettle from the hedgerow and find for himself if it had a sting. Wagers were laid and decided by the victim's silence or his sudden sharp intake of breath and muffled curse.

The English Milord was present, with a certain unsmiling coldness and he offered to prove the wagers another way. He beckoned Connie. The young Asian woman approached. I heard later that he had once encountered her before her life as a concubine began and that she had spurned his admiration. Perhaps that explained his conduct now.

"Put yourself over my knee, face down, Connie," he said quietly.

There was a look of apprehension in Connie's almond eyes as she obeyed him, the black silken hair hanging downward, her trim saffron-satin seat-cheeks facing upward. Now it was Connie who must make the wager, guessing the effect of each plucked nettle in turn. If she won, her reward was to be fed from the whisky flask. If she lost, she must endure the return of the last nettle to cause a gasp.

First she guessed it would not sting. The young man held the frond to her buttocks with no effect. One of his companions told the girl to turn her pretty face upwards, whereupon he held the whisky flask to her mouth. We saw her swallow once or twice, then make as if to turn her head away. He restrained this.

"A little more yet, Connie. We must fortify you for your ordeal!"

The man across whose knees she lay circled her waist with his left arm to hold her firmly. In his right hand he took another nettle, which Connie also pronounced harmless. This time she was wrong. As son as he touched the spiked leaf to the demure saffron cheek of her bottom, the Asian girl cried out her mistake, her trim legs twisting to no avail. The young man continued to hold the leaf to the same place until the allotted time was up. A deep pinkness the size of a large coin appeared on Connie's left buttock, with two or three white sting points in it.

Then came the forfeit. Was it pure malice which made the young man touch the virulent sharpness to that same tender place, holding it there with lips so tight that the veins on his forehead stood out? That done, he looked down at the appealing innocence of Connie's charming Chinese bottom. With no hint of amusement, he chose another frond, identical to that just discarded. Connie made a submissive, imploring sound, for rebellion is not in her nature.

Just then we were invited to witness Ibrahim's garden outing. The young man who was engaged with Connie remained deaf to this invitation. We left him still holding the Asian girl over his knee, not guessing what his eventual purpose might be. Looking back, I caught a glimpse of her face turning upward to him, its demure Oriental charm contorted into a devil mask of tears.

You will believe, Charlie, that all this was done merely to avenge himself in one way upon Connie. I assure you that you are wrong. The cunning secret, they tell me, is that such applications of nettles add much to one's enthusiasm for love. Connie well knew that by enduring such a preliminary she might hope for a rich harvest!

We came down to the lakeside pathway where there stood the strangest little equipage. It was a light garden carriage with shafts. Across these shafts were two securely fastened crossbars, one at the very front and another mid-way. From the direction of the house, two of Ibrahim's valets were escorting a loud-mouthed, strident youngster whom I believe you may well recognise.

She walked with a contemptuous toss of the long, fair hair, which framed the broad oval of her face, combed from a central parting to lie loose on her shoulders. Certainly the narrow eyes and thin mouth completed a picture of snub-nosed insolence.

Can this be the young hoyden you once spoke of? While not particularly tall or plump, Elaine appeared a sturdy enough adolescent in her white blouse and tie, the pleated grey skirt worn scandalously short in a brazen display of robust young thighs.

There was no doubt of her rebellious nature, which was visible in her strident manner and the toss of her fair hair, as well as audible in her vulgar speech. When she was given her orders at the carriage, she looked with contempt at the guests, undid her skirt and stepped out of it.

Because Ibrahim prefers such pupils to show their bare legs in brief dancing skirts, Elaine's schoolgirl knickers were no more than a pair of briefs in white stretched cotton. Her strong young hips and bottom-cheeks were thus admirably shaped for our observation.

She stood between the shafts, her back to the driver's seat of the little carriage. The harnessing began. Elaine had to bend forward over the first bar, which supported her young belly. A broad, stout strap was riveted to the bar and the valets now drew this tightly 'round Elaine's waist. Not only did it hold her down. By pressing her belly even more firmly on the bar, it caused her waist to arch downward and so increased the swell of Elaine's bottom in her tight knickers.

Her arms were at full stretch in front of her, each wrist securely held in a leather cuff to the front of the shaft. For the first time the impudence in the broad oval of her face and features seemed to falter.

She saw one of the valets take a slim cane with a spring like a rapier. He laid it conveniently by the driver's seat, adding a birch and one or two other means of discipline.

Elaine tossed her fair hair clear, and craned 'round with desperate anxiety to watch these preparations. She was gnawing compulsively at her lower lip in apprehension. Her hands were clenched into tight fists and her bare legs shifted and tensed as the men kept her waiting.

A still heat pervaded the afternoon. In the deep shade where we stood only the drone of insects disturbed the silence. The velvet petals of the red flowers seemed to wilt and the lake lay bright as a burning mirror. With loving slowness, one of the valets took the waistband of Elaine's knickers and pulled the little pants down her legs until she could step free of them. There was another stir of interest at this. While the youngster still watched us over her shoulder, we moved a little closer to take advantage of this bare rear view. Though I can only speak from a feminine point of view, Charlie, even I could see what it was that attracted the gentlemen of the party. Firmly broadened and rounded by her posture, the pale, sturdy cheeks of Elaine Cox's tomboy bottom had that robust, vulgar appeal which is perhaps at perfection in a girl of fifteen. The light-haired love-pouch peeped backward between her thighs; like her well-parted buttocks, it was within fondling distance of the driver.

One detail marred this charming cameo. The white tail of the school blouse still trailed slantwise across her bare seat. The valet now tucked it up, well clear of Elaine's young backside.

She appeared quite a big-bottomed girl in this posture, of course, and it was hard whether to think of her as pupil or woman. I imagine it is the fate of such a tomboy that her vigour and vulgarity lose her all consideration from the protective instincts of mankind. Certainly there was no suggestion on this occasion that she should be treated otherwise than a grown woman—nor any justification for that. Elaine was such a provoking mixture: the broad-hipped vulgarity of her backside in its present posture, the insolence of her manner, her schoolgirl tie and bare bottom, the impudence of a slut and the innocent awkwardness of adolesence.

Ibrahim appeared, applauded by the onlookers, who lined the lakeside path. He bowed to either side with gracious condescension. The greeting was returned. Then, turning in our direction, his eyes brightened at the sight of a bare-bottomed tomboy like Elaine harnessed bending between his carriage shafts. He took his place in the driver's seat. Elaine tossed her fair hair and craned 'round again, trying to watch him, with narrow-eyed anger.

Ibrahim leant forward a little. In his hands he seemed to weigh the full, pale schoolgirl bum-cheeks. Slowly his fingers moved.

"Such a warm little pouch," he murmured, "such sweltering lips! How many lucky young boys have been permitted a glimpse of it—and more. Back here, though, I sense a virginity. How tight! Even to the finger!"

Elaine twisted her hips as violently as the waist strap would allow. "You brute!" Hair tossing, face craning 'round, she vented her fury. "You dirty, filthy brute!"

Ibrahim sat back with a gentle sigh. "Such rebelliousness, Elaine? We must overcome that. Forward, if you please!"

As he spoke, Ibrahim took the slim cane in one

hand and tapped it into the palm of the other. Elaine's defiance was tinged with panic now, knowing the caning would begin as she moved forward.

"No!" The dismay and the rebellion were plainly heard in her cry. "I won't! No! No-o-o-o!"

Ibrahim smiled at the outburst. His arm went back. Down flashed the bamboo with a whip-like report across the sturdy, bare cheeks of Elaine Cox's fifteen-year-old bottom. What consternation in her eyes now! She bit her lip not to cry out, though her seat and thighs squirmed with anguish. She clearly regarded the humiliation of pony-girl discipline with a mixture of dread and defiance!

Ibrahim's smile broadened. He gave a second and third stroke of the cane across her young arse. His schoolgirl pony yelled wildly at the atrocious smart and tried to kick backwards. His mouth tightened in reproval. Karim, the valet, at his master's signal, cured this violence. He walked across, took the bamboo, and gave two thrashing strokes across the backs of Elaine's bare, sturdy thighs, keen enough to raise gooseflesh upon them.

What a change came over the young rebel now! The broad oval of Elaine's face was a picture of repentance. The narrow eyes brimmed with tears and the mouth wailed forlornly. She was almost more the whipped child of fifteen than the hardened young strumpet. Smiling, Ibrahim diddled her between her tomboy bottom-cheeks and thighs.

"Now your obedience training begins, Elaine Cox! You're sturdy enough to be my pony-girl—and impudent enough to need the whip across your bare bottom! Pull forward, Elaine!"

Smack! went the bamboo across her broad, young backside. 'Round went the wheels, with Elaine straining with every muscle of her robust young thighs and hips. The ornamental garden carriage trundled along the lakeside path, past banks of flowers rising like walls upon the dark-leaved shrubs.

Ibrahim had no eyes for the beauties of a garden. His gaze followed the squirming adolescent hips, the arching and rounding of Elaine's bum-cheeks, as she pulled forward. Her fatly offered adolescent seat bore the long, swelling weals of the bamboo's tapestry. At each step forward, with leg lifted, her hips went farther over the crossbar. With each stride, she lay almost bottom-upwards over the bar, buttocks enticingly parted in a full rear view. Elaine's backside tempted punishment like any fifth-form tomboy over the desk, awaiting the teacher's bamboo. The sight stiffened Ibrahim's disciplinary zeal. His cane rang out across the squirming, robust cheeks of Elaine's bottom, like a ringmaster's whip. Several times he required his minions to detain her in this pose while he added six or eight wicked strokes across the weals with which he had already embroidered Elaine's seat.

I will not weary you with an account of every detail. Suffice it to say that no act of a sexual nature was performed on this remarkable outing. The obedience lesson to which Elaine was submitted was, in essentials, of a kind thoroughly approved by England's moral educators.

As the sun waned over the pleasure gardens, the equipage came to an incline in the path, running up to the finest of the temples. Even a sturdy youngster of fifteen was tested in all her sinews to pull the carriage forward. Her momentum flatered. Ibrahim chose a woven, snakeskin pony-lash. *Smack!* went the whip across the broadened cheeks of Elaine's backside. Frantically she writhed her robust young thighs, struggling wildly upwards, arse over the harness bar. How seductively and lewdly Elaine's adolescent rump squirmed in this posture.

Ibrahim rose in his seat, teeth set with disciplinary zeal. *Smack*! The pony-lash sought the lower fatness of Elaine Cox's tomboy bottom-cheeks. Smack! Whip-smack! Whip-crack-smack! Surely her screams were justified by the ruby beads punctuating the lash marks, trickling down and spending themselves on her thighs.

I had some misgivings at the severity employed to ensure that she accomplished the last and most arduous part of her lesson. Yet one must consider Ibrahim's view. The slope of the path and the labour required caused the seat and hips of Elaine to arch out and squirm in the most lewd and tantalising manner. It almost seemed that Elaine was deliberately thrusting her fifteen-year-old backside in his face, arching and rounding its fattened cheeks at every step. As her sturdy young legs strained forward, she alternately showed the love-pouch at her thighs and then her widely opened arse-valley. No teacher who had Elaine bending thus before the class could resist giving exemplary chastisement for the moral improvement of the others.

A gate was closed across the path, its keeper standing by. Ibrahim diddled his finger impatiently between the buttocks of his sturdy fifth-form schoolgirl.

"Sound your little post-horn for the gate to open, Elaine!"

When she hesitated, a crack of the snakeskin lash across her bum-cheeks strengthened the force of the command. She was beyond modesty, anyhow. With a cry of compliance, Elaine Cox farted as only a vulgar tomboy of her age knew how. The witty gatekeeper chose to be deaf. Again the snakeskin kissed

Elaine's strapping young buttocks. She emitted two of the rudest carriage notes ever heard in the history of equitation. And so the gate opened.

So the obedience lesson ended. What controversies would attend it outside the harem walls! Yet it contained one advantage. Before it began, Elaine seemed a hard, impudent rebel. One felt pitiless in dealing with her, as if she were an insolent and vulgar grown woman of fifteen. Now the snub-nosed impudence of the broad oval of her face was dissolved in tears, she wailed for pity. Now one could soften towards her. She was a child, a schoolgirl of fifteen, pitilessly whipped for her offence. Of course one smiled and teased her gently about the whipping, to ensure that she did not forget its purpose. Yet now one could fondle Elaine gently and affectionately, knowing that she would respond with the tearful gratitude of a schoolgirl whipped and pardoned.

The two valets unfastened her and led her away. Elaine walked with her skirt and knickers in her hand, unable to wear them in her present state. The forlorn young mouth relaxed from its sobbing dejection and the weeping was less copious. Her head was still bowed a little in self-pity, her gentler wailing accompanied by the brushing-away tears with the edge of her hand. She walked slowly and uncomfortably. One could not begin to count the number of swollen weals from the bamboo that crossed her tomboy buttocks.

As she passed the onlookers, Ibrahim explained that another such punishment lesson would be given her in a few weeks' time.

You may imagine Elaine looking 'round at us, the broad oval of her face a study in dismay, as she tossed back her long fair hair. Make no mistake, several of the spectators craned forward to catch her gaze. It seems they wanted Elaine to see their eyes wide and mouths open in amazement and delight at what was going to happen to her.

Do you deplore this as the vindictive lechery of the harem? Believe me, Charlie, it is no less common among our educators and moralists at home. As Lord Byron remarks to them when they execute vengeance upon a pair of shapely buttocks, " 'Tis well your cassocks hide your rising lust." Had you but seen the sight in the reformatory punishment room on the night before Elaine was shipped into harem slavery, you would need no further argument. On that last evening, she was strapped over the block on all fours, as if for judicial caning. The justices sat smiling in their chairs to watch. The master, grave-faced in his shirtsleeves, carried the bamboo.

You might have thought it a lesson in moral dis-cipline. And so it was but for one thing. Elaine would be going to a place from which she would never return to tell tales! All restraint upon the mor-alists was removed. It was a year ago when she had much the appearance she has now.

The eight magistrates were rotund figures of about fifty. They went in two by two at first. Elaine's skirt and pants were lowered. By talk of whips and cigar tips, she was made compliant. One man knelt before her and she sucked his grey-haired cock. The other knelt at the rear, seduced by the full, pale cheeks of Elaine Cox's fourteen-year-old bottom. Four in suc-cession sodomised the schoolgirl tomboy, four more obliging her to swallow love's potion. Her virginity was kept for the market-place.

Three dozen with the cane across her sturdy, bare backside. Then, since no one would ever know, the pony-lash! A savage half-hour. Elaine Cox, scream-ing and twisting, saw only stiff, grey-haired pricks and smiles of delight. Such is the influence of moral discipline! Lads from the adjoining boys' reformatory risked life and limb, shinning up to peer in at the high, barred windows. As the thirty-six allotted bamboo strokes were given across the cheeks of Elaine's arse, the lads grinned knowingly at her. She was the permitted spy at their masturbation rituals, the young slut who sucked off the winner of the bare-knuckle boxing. When, her buttocks wealed by the bamboo, the whip was chosen in addition, not one of them would have gone to her aid. They too were longing to see Elaine taken all the way into that darker region which lies far beyond the limit of any punishment. To her screams as her bottom was skinned they replied with priapic delirium, each lad pumping his organ until his eyes rolled back and the gruel jetted wildly out. Was this truly superior to the example of the harem?

At dinner we were waited upon by two of Ibrahim's fourteen-year-old nymphs. Valerie was a slim gamine, with a short, auburn crop and a slender figure. Linda appeared so a soft, sensuous little blonde, with sly, blue eyes, a short mane of fair hair, and a sniggering manner. I cannot say which of these two slipped a note under my plate informing me that they and other beauties had been abducted and were now unwilling bed slaves of the pasha. I was beseeched to convey this news to London. A gunboat might then blast the palace of Ibrahim to pieces and carry home the little minxes in triumph!

Be sure I know my duty! I handed the note to Ibrahim at once. He thanked me gravely, promising me that, in the coming night, Linda and Valerie should be birched for five minutes each time the clock struck. I begged only that he would make it ten minutes!

You approve my action, Charlie? Think what a scandal would result from the note writen by these little sluts! The pashas are our loyalist allies! Imagine the fate of poor Papa—and he only just accoutred with an ambassador's cocked hat and plumes! Britannia may have her faults, but she knows better than lesser nations the importance of avoiding such imprudent disclosures!

I was not much disturbed that night by agreeable images of the plump, pearly little moons of Linda's bottom under the bamboo. It is no worse than discipline in many an English home. Thus I take my adoring leave of you, dearest Charlie. Your next news is eagerly awaited by

Your ever-loving Lizzie

My own dearest Lizzie,

MY HEART leapt for joy when an envelope came bearing upon it your own unmistakable hand. I read your bold account of the good Sultan Ibrahim and his novel method of carriage propulsion! It is true, my sweet, there are young termagants like Elaine who, by every moral right, should be put to discipline of this kind. Almost all the educators and justices of England would agree with me in that.

By the same token, one respects a wife who is loyal to her husband and duties. Once she transgresses, however, is there any reason for trying to shield her from the ravishing of the world?

In my own small way, I too have had a victory over a recalcitrant girl. I speak of our young trollop Noreen. But what insolence still dwells in those hard, pale features and brown eyes.

The other night, Miss Martinet, aided by her staff, was awarding discipline to certain strapping young wenches like Noreen. The procedure for this is, indeed, singular. There is a long bench over which the

girls kneel, presenting a row of tightly clad backsides. Their wrists are strapped to a rail on the far
side, so that they kneel over the bench on all fours.
Lastly, a long screen is lowered from a rail to the
backs of their waists, so that they cannot see who
stands behind them.

That night it was Miss Martinet who walked down
the row. She indicated the fate of each delinquent,
for the benefit of the grooms, by chalking on the
tightly clad seat-cheeks. Thus a number chalked on
the left cheek indicated strokes to be given by the
person responsible. A number on the other half
showed the preliminary to be given by a groom with
a gym-shoe heel.

I vowed to curb Noreen's ill-mannered conduct.
So, as Miss M. walked down the line, I watched
closely. She strolled up and down the row several
times. Pausing she applied the chalk to the robust
young cheeks of Maggie's seat and inscribed the
numbers "20" and "12." A moment more and she
drew "30" and "12" where a pair of tight, grey pants
was strained over the full, young cheeks of Susan
Underwood's bottom. Sue, with her soft, blond
beauty, was a girl whom it would be a pleasure to get
into trouble. So it went on until the tour of duty was
complete. To my dismay, however, Noreen was un-
chalked!

The remedy for that was simple. The curtain had
been arranged so that the culprits could not see who
was chalking them. It was also intended to prevent a
groom with a grude from adding to the punishment
of a girl with whom he had a quarrel. In this case,
however, Noreen was easily identifiable. The collar
length of her dark hair was concealed as she lay over
the bench. Yet, in kneeling over it, she offered an
unmistakable alternative profile. The pale jeans seat

was taut across her firm, statuesque buttocks, the central seam drawn taut and deep into her arse-crack. The lower softness of her bum-cheeks almost closing over the seam could belong to only one of the miscreants.

I stood there, as if I might Miss M., or whoever had been deputed to this task. Then I ran a hand over the thin, taut denim, which sheathed Noreen's backside. As I did so, she caught her breath, knowing that she was about to be marked with the chalk which lay conveniently to hand. Under my stroking hand I could feel the tensing of her buttocks and her taut, young thighs.

Perhaps it was because she had believed herself safe, having escaped the weekly reckoning, that she now reacted with such consternation. I ran a hand between the rear opening of her thighs and gave her cunt-pouch a good feel through the tight cloth. I continued so long that I began to feel Noreen moistening herself in the clinging pants despite her predicament.

I drew my hand away and left her in suspended animation, so near and yet so far from her fulfilment. My hands were now busy again with the firm, sturdy cheeks of Noreen's arse, stroking, parting, and thumbing. She pushed back impatiently with her hips but, much as she urged it, she could not quite bring herself to beg for the masturbation to continue.

Then I took the chalk, and she was tense and still so that she would be able to feel the shape of the numbers written. On one cheek, I wrote "12" for the groom with the hard-heeled rubber gym-slipper. Noreen cried out, "No!" in a protest at this preliminary discipline. Then, on the other cheek, I chalked a "36." She cried out in alarm, for she had good reason to know what that would mean.

Greatly looking forward to the night ahead, I now

tiptoed away to my room and awaited events. I sat in the easy chair, reading the fancies of the *Sporting Times* and smoking a thoughtful pipe, as if I had been there all the evening.

Presently I was aware of a disturbance in the next room, to which the grooms had taken my culprit. Noreen still displayed her firm-faced indifference, no more than a flick of her dark fringe or a stare from her impudent brown eyes. They had, I think, held her over a tall stool with her pants undone and pulled down to her ankles.

From the gasping and protests I concluded that one of them was fiddling with her as she was secured. They could not, of course, unbutton themselves and do what they wanted in this situation. Yet it was impossible to believe that they would not play "dirty girl" between her legs with their fingers and between the cheeks of her backside.

The laughter and smiling stopped. One groom spat lightly on the rubber gym-shoe heel. There was a *whack*! and a *smack*! To judge from the sharp intake of breath, it had stung her hard, for her pale bottom-cheeks were jumping and quivering like spanked jelly under the impacts.

One could tell that Noreen was biting her lip not to cry out, as if seeking to deny the groom his triumph over her. He, on the other hand, was grinning back at her, sensing his victory in her tensing seat-cheeks and loud, uneven breath. She held out as the gym-slipper tanned her twice more, and then let out a long gasp.

"Now the first cheek all over again, Noreen," smiled the groom. "No, don't squirm your seat like that, you young trollop! We'll see to it that Mr. Charles's cane has something to work on!"

I gathered that even when the discipline was finished there was further hostility. A sound of struggling was caused by one groom working the singlet up in order to play with Noreen's tits. The other positively could not draw his fingers away from between her legs and bum-cheeks.

At last they brought her in, wearing only the white singlet, which ended at her waist. In the customary manner, she was made to stand in the corner with her back to the room like a spanked schoolgirl in disgrace. She was not permitted to speak until spoken to, nor to move until ordered to do so. I was to keep her there in that posture until it was convenient for me to complete the discipline. Her wrists were strapped together in front of her, but she was not otherwise restrained.

So I sat there and read the racing column over and over while I smoked a pipe and drank another glass of hock and seltzer. Or so it appeared. In truth, for the next half hour or more, my eyes peeped over the edge of the *Sporting Times*. I simply could not draw my gaze from the deliciously provoking view which a young slut like Noreen offers in this situation. To keep her waiting was also a means of heightening the drama—comedy or tragedy, according to one's view. They had left the stout, leather belt of her riding jeans strapped tightly 'round her waist, narrowing her there and emphasising the proud swell of her hips and seat.

What was rather appealing was the way in which she stood with head bowed, the dark hair just lifted clear of her collar at the back. I was able to admire her strong and straight young back, the firm robust young thighs, the cheeks of her well-made bottom, still blushing deeply from her tanning and marked in several places by the muddy print of the gym-shoe heel.

I noticed that, as a half-hour ended, Noreen grew increasingly restive. How shall I describe it? Her thighs seemed to shift and tense together a little. The cheeks of her bottom pressed together spasmodically, reducing her arse-cleft to a thin, tight line.

I stood up and walked across to reprimand such willful disobedience. "You were ordered to stand *still*, Noreen! Since you seem to find such difficulty in obeying a simple command, we must enforce that instruction with the cane! Perhaps that will cure you of fidgeting. Bend over! Right over! Do you hesitate, you young slut? Obey the command! At once!"

Rather awkwardly, as it seemed to me, and breathing audibly, Noreen bent to touch her toes. I went down on one knee behind her and my hands made a brief but intimate examination of her strapping young backside. Then I turned away to take the cane from its cupboard.

As I did so, I heard from behind me the sound of a loud and vulgar raspberry. I swung 'round. I must admit that Noreen, her mouth open in alarm, did not look like a girl who had just pressed her tongue between her lips and blown off that street-urchin rudeness. Yet I can hardly believe that my ears deceived me at such close range! Moreover, the young strumpet certainly showed open defiance. Though her pale, firm-featured face was suffused with consternation, she had straightened up and was standing with one hand pressed to her behind. I had certainly given no permission for such a change in posture.

"Very well, Noreen," I said quietly, "if you will have it so, you will. I should very much like to give your backside a long session with the pony-lash tonight. Unfortunately, such extreme discipline must be approved by Miss Martinet. Be assured I shall apply to her in the morning. Tonight you shall have the cane."

In order that I might enjoy the retribution fully, I thought it prudent to require her to pull her pants up and to have her escorted to the stable-block, well out of earshot. Would I not be approved of by those passing admirers who had seen the strapping young wench standing slack-hipped as a whore? When the grooms had secured her on all fours over the padded birching stool, would not those admirers have stood agog at the same sight? The pale-blue jeans seat was splitting tight over the strong, well-made cheeks of Noreen's backside. A flick of her dark hair and she was staring back with the same firm-faced impudence which had greeted their admiration of her in this pose.

I undid her at the waist and pushed the pants to her knees, adding one more strap to pinion her sturdy legs together just at the base of her thighs. My finger teased the rear pout of her vaginal lips. My hands fondled the pale, sturdy swell of her bottom-cheeks. My finegrs fiddled remorselessly between those cheeks for several minutes, despite the tensing and shifting of her seat.

"Thirty-six strokes of the bamboo across your behind, Noreen. That is your allotted penalty for a week's misconduct. After that, we must add something for your disgraceful conduct in the other room."

Now, under the level fringe of dark hair, her eyes filled with dismay. Yet I had endured enough of her impudence and was resolved.

"You fear you will not be able to bear it, Noreen? Fortunately, the choice is not yours. You will be made to bear it all the same."

She could not take her eyes off the long, rippling

bamboo. I was determined to subdue her quickly. She gave a gasp of fright as I measured the first stroke very low, across the light creases which divided Noreen's statuesque buttocks and thighs, a supremely sensitive area.

"Six strokes in succession across there, Noreen, to teach you manners!"

The first lash of the bamboo across that path made her fingers clench and thighs press hard together. A flat *smack*! of the cane across the same track brought a half-suppressed cry. With wicked but righteous accuracy, I landed two more on top of those. Noreen screamed as the last two whipped the swelling bamboo print of the others.

"And two more across there, Noreen. Just where the edge of the chair comes. Remember this when next you are tempted to be insolent."

Twice more I caught her there. Noreen's bottom-cheeks were writhing, as if she were seated bare on a red-hot saddle. What a tale of woe might be read in that hard young face now; Noreen's tears were brimming and coursing down. I touched the cane across the crowns of her buttocks, where she was so broad.

"Eight strokes here, Noreen. Right where you sit."

Wide-eyed and wild-mouthed, she made the rafters ring. I allowed her a pause after the second batch. Then I put my lips to her ear.

"And now, Noreen, your thirty-six."

At nineteen, Noreen is so strongly built I quite thought she would break the straps in her frenzy at learning this. But they held her. I continued to murmur to her—for my bark was to prove worse then my bite—explaining the leniency of such discipline. There were countries in the world, I told her, where such insolence by a slave girl to her master would be rewarded by one last night. There, too, she would be on all fours, though strapped down astride the traditional bench, her thighs conveniently parted and rump-cheeks spread. The grave-faced vizier would watch the two burly, lion-clothed minions during the long night. The whips and the implements of the brazier would be eagerly employed upon Noreen's bottom there, no less than between her thighs. Monstrous devices would impale her both ways. Without remorse, dawn would bring the belly skewer to nineteen-year-old Noreen and the leather collar would be tightened inexorably. The final scene would reveal Noreen tumbled arse-upwards in a dark pit, the food for predators.

Such words do more good than all the canes in the world. With the thrashing at last finished, I undid the straps which held her ankles and legs.

If you imagine her lashing back at me with her feet kicking wildly, you are quite wrong. Noreen set her knees wide apart with frantic haste, thrust her hips back, and begged for love in the humblest and most pleading terms. She sobbed for it, if only as a temporary respite from correction. What could I do? Laying down the cane I knelt behind her and unbuttoned myself. Then my stiffness parted the way through her love-pouch from behind and into her warm, receptive depths. Gently at first, then harder, we rode together until the bomb of passion burst and I flooded her most copiously.

How she feared now that the caning might resume! Lowering her shoulders and straight dark hair, she raised her seat and begged for love another way. When I said that she deserved to be caned for suggesting such a thing, she pleaded all the harder, most vulgarly offering me her "arse" and promising "a good time" with it.

My finger soaped her tight portal of Sodom. "Too

late to recant now, Noreen!" I said, smiling at her. "Will you still think it worth the excitement when I cane you for this afterwards? Now lie more tightly over the scroll."

I did not, of course, punish her as I threatened. Taking her breasts in my hands as the guide, I rode Noreen's arse in the grand manner, spending copiously inside it. When it was over, she knew that the caning might follow. I could scarcely believe her next request. I undid her and staggered to the chair, from which I have not had the strength to rise since being squeezed from Noreen's rear. Yet I gave my consent to her suggestion. As I pen these last lines, she kneels before me and takes in her mouth my stiffening. . . . My darling Lizzie, I can write no further. . . . Ah, Noreen, you delicious young whore! Your tongue—use it again like that! Ah! . . .

Believe me, Lizzie, your own adoring Charles. . . . A leather strap round your throat, Noreen, that I may guide you by its reins. . . . Rise now, turn, and bend. . . . Sit upon the love-lance. . . . Deep in your behind. Noreen! . . Move up and down gently. . . . And thus, my sweet Lizzie. . . . Harder, Noreen, you young bitch!

31 July 1904

My darling Lizzie,

CATASTROPHE HAS come upon us! I write at the first opportunity, knowing not where I am, and having only a general notion of the day of the month.

You will scarcely believe what has occurred—the audacity and the impudence of the young whore who has brought such things about! When I wrote my last adoring letter to you, I was, you may well believe, in a state of nervous excitement after my night of fun with Noreen. I was still lightly distracted and, therefore, made a fair copy of the letter in which I corrected all those small errors one makes under such circumstances. The rough copy, with all its blots and scorings out, I discarded in the waste-paper basket. Why did I not burn it—I would surely have done so within the hour?

I went to post my letter to you. When I returned, the basket had been emptied by the servant, and the paper had gone. I thought no more of this. What could it matter? On the following day, Miss Martinet and I received a visitor—an inspector of constabulary! Noreen, in a wild passion of vengeance for being thrashed, had stolen the copy of my letter and smuggled it out to the local newspaper! The proprietor of the paper, an officious penny-a-liner oaf, had gone with it to the police station!

Here was a pretty pickle! The inspector was friendship itself, and most respectful to one of my standing in society.

"The pity of it is, sir," he said, supping the tea which Miss Martinet had poured, "that something cannot be done about such young whores as Noreen! They get above themselves and imagine it is their privilege to abuse their superiors! If I had my way, such sluts would be taken to the strictest prison and there birched raw twice a week. If they were never set at liberty to make mischief again, it would not greatly trouble me."

This gave me hopes that I should come off well.

"Unfortunately, sir," he went on, "now that this has come to the notice of the newspaper and the police, it cannot well be ignored. If there were any way to prevent it coming to court, it should be done. Alas, sir, it cannot now be done. Even without any generous consideration from yourself and Miss Martinet, I would strive to prevent it. But that is beyond my power now. Be sure we shall have our eyes upon the newspaper fellow and shall prosecute him at the first chance. But what good will that do you, sir?"

I opened my pocket-book, drew out several bank notes, and made his visit well worth his while. Next day came Colonel Whackford, the chief constable of the county. He was full of the same regrets.

"There must be a prosecution, Mr. Charles," he said, shaking his old grey head sadly, "but count upon me for one thing. It shall be delayed a day or two. Make the best of your chance. It would be a timely thing if you could manage to make yourself scarce the next two or three years. The young bitch who caused the trouble might also be transferred elsewhere."

The chairman of the local justices also paid us a call—going away with his pockets fuller. Wringing his hands, he swore that next day he would be obliged to sign a warrant for my arrest and another for Noreen's detention as a witness. He had tried to prevent this but the Lord Chancellor, his master, had been adamant. It was not that the Lord Chancellor too could not be bribed—being only a politician, after all—but rather that his price came too steep for us.

Next morning, Miss Martinet told me to pack my things at once: the officers of the law were coming for me. I was to be taken in custody to the Isle of Wight, where there was a prison for such creatures as I until the time of our trial. Certain of the girls from Greystones were to be sent to a reformatory in the same neighbourhood, it seemed, and would be accompanied by the officers.

The inspector arrived. He arrested me with so many winks and nods that I thought him nervously afflicted. Two constables escorted Noreen, Vanessa, Jackie, Julie, and several other delinquents to the large, closed van. Thus I took a final fond farewell of Greystones and Miss Martinet. You may be sure I distributed all my remaining funds to the officers of the law—twenty each to the two constables and fifty sovs for the inspector.

Deuced civil they were in return, providing food and glasses of dark, foaming ale on the way. The inspector confided to me that Noreen's treason had been carried by Vanessa. I looked at her. For the convenience of the journey she had been put aboard in the white singlet and tight, blue ruding jeans which she had been wearing when summoned. No sign now of the innocent-looking blouse, tie, and demure skirt of her uniform.

There was still, I thought, a mockery in the face of this fourth-form schoolgirl! The brown hair worn straight to the collar with parted fringe was not unlike Noreen's, as if she aped the older girl. What of the firm, lightly sunbrowned face, with its clear-cut features, high cheekbones, and laughing blue eyes? Such innocence indeed!

As if to pile misery upon me, the inspector—with the nervous wink and nod of a man in the grip of St. Vitus jig—assured me that Vanessa must receive a reward for her cleverness. How downcast this left me! Presently the inspector said we must stop, though I did not see why, for we were miles from anywhere, on a wooded road. All the girls but Vanessa were handcuffed to the detention rail in the van. The young traitress and one of the two constables got out with the inspector and me. Vanessa is not big-hipped or fat-bottomed at fourteen, but she has the slight ungainly puppy fat at the hips and the seat of a goose who has yet to become a swan. As I watched her walk into the trees, the pale-blue tightness of the riding jeans gave an almost slovenly weight to Vanessa's fourteen-year-old arse-cheeks, and to her hips generally.

It seems that the length of the journey had put Vanessa in the plight of a pupil kept in class too long by the teacher, and now needing to squat in the ladylike privacy of the trees and piss for a full minute or two. Imagine the desperate and vindictive mood I was in, Lizzie—as you would have been on my behalf. Given the chance I would have allowed Vanessa to remove her riding pants but not the tight, white-cotton knickers. Would I have allowed visits to the trees? Be sure I would not! I would have set up the folding table and made her lie on her side upon it, her back to the watching girls and officers, her hips and seat in the cotton pants arching towards them.

As a mere prelude to my vengeance, I would have commanded Vanessa to wet her pants in front of the onlookers, enforcing the injunction by tantalising the little water-spout between her legs with finger-tickling. She would soak herself before I was done. I imagine the officers, at least, would have been vastly intrigued to see this little temptress, though a grown-up, fourth form girl, wet her pants in this manner.

It was, of course, out of the question. The inspector and the constable led her to a place among the trees. I waited. Presently the inspector reappeared and summoned me with his nervous wink and jerk of the head. I followed him to a small opening among the trees—and what do you think I saw, Lizzie?

A tree had been felled across the glade—a stout trunk. Vanessa was kneeling over it, still fully dressed, the tight and heavy-cheeked seat of her riding jeans well raised. She had not assumed the posture voluntarily for the constable knelt with her shoulders clamped between his burly thighs. The obliging inspector cut a long, slim switch from an ash sapling and handed it to me.

"Take your time, sir," he said courteously, "we need not resume our journey just yet. If I may be so bold as to suggest, Vanessa's bum-cheeks will be more responsive if bare. I feel sure that would be the wish of a teacher at her school."

I was, you may imagine, flabbergasted by the suggestion. Though I had paid the officers of the law handsomely, I had never supposed I would be given this last liberty of taking revenge upon the little minxes who had brought me to this present pass. Yet, my dear Lizzie, you may believe that I was not slow to seize the opportunity.

Half-expecting them to stop me, I undid the riding jeans and tugged them awkwardly to her knees. Vanessa twisted a little, but the constable's hold of her shoulders was strong and secure. Vanessa's knickers were, indeed, the tight, schoolgirl kind of white cotton. I lowered these too, noting how she tensed against the intrusion of fingers inside her pants! I was more than a little nervous, never having had to deal with an adolescent girl pupil before. I craned my head down and examined the slight adolescent heaviness, the almost muddy pallor of Vanessa's fourth-form bottom! To prevent wriggling, I drew off my belt and strapped her legs together just above the knees, then trussed her ankles with another lent by the inspector. Her light-haired young cunt was just peeping between her thighs. There was no point—and indeed no time—to lecture the delinquent on her offence. I warned her briefly.

"You know you're going to have your arse thrashed, Vanessa. For what you've done, you must be hurt, and, believe me, you will be."

Can you imagine it, Lizzie? Such stern words from one whose life has been passed in pleasure. Ah, but life was pleasant no longer! I will not weary you with Vanessa's desperate pleading, the reasons advanced why she should not be whipped, her inability to endure it on her bare bottom, her urgent need to let her fountain gush, her promises to be good, never to offend again. Urged on by the officers of the law, I touched the ash switch across her squirming seat-cheeks, took aim, and thrashed hard.

For the next ten minutes, it was dance time for Vanessa, or at least for the adolescent puppy-fat cheeks of her muddy-white bottom. Her thighs are still quite slim, and I took care not to execute judgment upon them. Yet the taut elasticity of Vanessa's fourth-form bum-cheeks was severely dealt with. It is hard to judge, I suppose, when whipping the bare backside of a fourteen-year-old high-school girl on the frontier of sophistication and feminine beauty, whether to treat her as a young woman or a little girl. Had she not committed a woman's crime? Thinking of this I cast restraint aside and thrashed the slim switch across Vanessa's bottom-cheeks!

How she screamed! Yet I guessed the sly minx was acting a part. There were as yet only two raised and burning stripes across her innocently immature bum-cheeks—both marks low down—which convinced me that they had taken effect well. I resolved to ignore her hysterics, the wild promises of repentance and amendment, the shrill imploring of those, now miles away, who might save her from her fate. I would judge only by the state of Vanessa's arse-cheeks.

When I stopped, and looked at the inspector, he gave me a quizzical glance and directed my attention to Vanessa's behind, as if to say, "Finished already? Come, now! Please continue!" I think there were three rather stiff members in that woodland glade at the sight of Vanessa's backside being tanned! So I gave her a last bout, first stooping to her ear.

"Since I shall soon be within prison walls, Vanessa, and since you will have helped to put me there, I want you to know that I am enjoying thrashing your bottom very much indeed. Now, much worse this time!"

When it was over, Vanessa was allowed into the trees for a weep, a gulping of final tears, and a release of bladder water. I was gratified that she preferred to complete the journey in the van without her pants on and sitting sideways on her hip.

So we came safe, in the arms of the law, to the prison ferry at Portsmouth. The young female delinquents were taken aboard. Before I started down the gangway, the two constables saluted me smartly, congratulated me again on the striping and bruising of Vanessa's bottom, and thanked me for my "great generosity" to them. The inspector came aboard as my escort.

It was now dark, yet I was surprised how gaily lit the prison ferry seemed to be. It had the size and look of an ocean-going steam-yacht. The inspector escorted me to a comfortable chair in the forward saloon and commanded a hock and seltzer for me from a warder who looked for all the world like a mess steward. I began to hope that my sentence might be served in such agreeable conditions. I asked the inspector the name of this prison hulk.

"Do you not know, sir?" said he, "it is the steam-yacht *Brandon*."

You being less of a duffer than I, Lizzie, will have guessed the truth ere now. My wily Uncle Brandon had seen just such a difficulty as mine and had laid his plans. Not only did he enjoy the Greystones girls but contrived to ship many of them to lands where harem beauties are bought on the auction block! Thus he had made his fortune and, with the cargo I now possessed, he put me in the way of making my own. As for the inspector, Uncle Brandon had bought him as a mere constable. The zealous officer had, many a time, acted as master of ceremonies on these occasions.

I vow, Lizzie, to tell the story of my escape thus far exhausts me. Forgive me, my dearest, if I now take a fond leave of you and lay my head for the night on the pillow of a fugitive.

And so the morning comes and finds me refreshed again. I have husbanded my energies in order to tell you the most comical thing that ever happened to me. Whoever the fellow was who said that life at sea is worse than confinement in prison would eat his words if could see me now.

On our first day out, I cast an eye upon the girls to see which should divert me between the sheets during our voyage. I was rather taken with Julie, nineteen years old. Do you recall her? She it was who sucked old Silas Raven while he watched Vanessa do her naked dance in Miss Martinet's music room.

I chose a morning when she was ordered to don her singlet and working trousers for deck-washing. How well one could observe her now. Unlike Vanessa, a little girl with a woman's appeal, Julie is petite and slim—a woman in child's shape. With tall heels on her shoes, she is still diminutive. Her golden-blond hair is worn in a loose sweep from her high crown, lying on her back to the top of her shoulder blades. A somewhat sulky little face is marked by rather a crude nose and weak chin, hazel eyes with darkened lashes.

She is, to talk colloquially, what is known as a penis-teaser. The blue denim of the working trousers is worn tight and smooth as a skin. One views, as if she were naked, the slender thighs, which, even at their tops, are scarcely thicker than a man's upper arm. She has that taut belly and backward jut of hips which is characteristic of girl children rather than young women. Her breasts are small and her bottom, though its cheeks are quite slim and tightly rounded, has a soft, feminine fatness in proportion to her other curves.

Thus I watched her. To speak the truth, the tight denim trousers were not entirely smooth. The straining of the skin-tight denim caused sheaves of creases across the backs of her knees and, indeed, across the backs of her childishly slim upper thighs. The tight seam under her legs visibly parted her love-lips. I have read somewhere of girls who can frig themselves by the tightness of such clothes. Did Julie masturbate on the cord seam as she walked? When she bent over, her bottom-cheeks became two tight, distinct rounds with a deep and widely open arse-valley between. What a sight if the denim trousers had not impeded the view!

Yet to what purpose was all this? Who would bed a sulky little penis-teaser for preference? I said as much to the inspector. He at once promised me that Julie should prove as eager to please me as if her life depended on it, but he would not tell me why or how. Believe this who may, says I to myself! Yet, in the course of the day, I caught many a flutter from the lashes of those dark, hazel eyes, and often a vacant, hopeful smile. How was this, I wondered?

Late that night, I rang the bell in my cabin for my brandy and soda. Instead of the steward, it was Julie who tiptoed in, darkened eyelashes fluttering. The sulky little face made a visible effort to be alluring. As I tossed back my brandy, she stood before me, squirming her tight-denimed thighs together—indeed frigging herself on the seam!—giving out imploring little sighs and whimpers. Next she perched on my knee, thighs still squirming, and led my hand under the gusset of her pants.

"Please!" It was a little girl's whimpering half-sob, demanding to be indulged.

"Get your pants off, then, Julie! Astride my thighs, facing me, as I sit here! That way you'll get the shaft nice and deep between your legs!"

How eagerly she stripped off her pants? Julie's knickers came next, and she gingerly lowered herself onto the erection. How she rode! As if her life indeed depended on winning this race! Jig! Jig! Jig! she went, rising and falling in the saddle like a true equestrienne. Her tongue was more active in my mouth than almost any other girl I have encountered. Nor was this a single bout. After the first pumping of my lust into Julie's cunt, we retired to the bed and there repeated the rogering of her love-pouch three times during the night in various postures.

I was not surprised when she appeared the next night, though a surprise was indeed in store. When I suggested a repetition, a cunt-ride on the prick, Julie gave a sulky little wail.

"We did that last night!"

Never before had I heard that such things were allowed on one night only. A moment more, however, and she was on her knees before me, unbuttoning my trousers. Though Julie's knickers came off, she would do nothing but suck the penis and swallow its tribute, which she did twice more during the night.

The third evening, she would do nothing but make love to herself for my diversion, her bare thighs wide open, knees bent, the nails of her slim fingers painted so that the effect of her masturbation was more dramatic.

On the fourth night, she again insisted on something new. How long could this continue? Turning her back to my chair, she bent over, and I admired the tight, denim seat moulding her taut, well-separated bum-cheeks and the open valley between. So that I might see her face better, I made her plait her hair and pin it in a top-knot. What a little madam she looked! Off came the pants and knickers. She bent with knees tucked a little forward and parted. The tight, slim cheeks of her bottom, her narrow hips, the dark anus-bud, seemed so fragile to look at. Prudently, I took a slim, glass pencil-squirt of liquid soap, inserted it in Julie's behind, and pressed the bulb, giving her half an hour of in-and-out with the slender rod.

"I fear I must stretch you hard now, Julie," I said, adjusting my stiffness to her. Then presently, "I think you like a man to bugger you, don't you, Julie? You know you're going to a harem master? The man who's bought you will give you plenty of this!"

Once again, the pleasure was repeated during the night.

The mystery grew deeper. Next night, Julie came to my cabin but resisted all my approaches. This was too much! I seized her wrist as I sat there and so drew her forcibly to kneel by my chair. Gently but deliberately, she twisted her head, set her pretty little teeth to my wrist, and bit me softly. As she did so, the dark hazel eyes looked up at me.

"I must be whipped for that!" she said quietly.

Before I could deny it, she had gone to the cupboard and come back with a single-cord whip, some two feet long. She handed it to me, took off her pants and knickers again, and bent over, her slim buttocks tightly and separately rounded. She had chosen to bend over a tall stool equipped with attaching-straps. In this posture too I required her mane of blond hair to be plaited and pinned in a top-knot that I might see her young face more easily. Seen from the rear, her thighs seemed almost fragile in their slenderness. The neat, demure cheeks of Julie's nineteen-year-old bottom were tightly rounded and well parted as a result of her petite shape. She had chosen to bend diagonally over the top of the stool—corner to corner—which seemed unusual. Yet what difference could it make, since the straps held her arms and legs so tightly?

"I shall make a note for the pasha who has bought you, Julie," I said, "recommending frequent harem discipline on those bare bum-cheeks of yours."

I thought she might be grateful—even excited. But she cried in her whining voice, "No! Please, don't do that! Oh, please!"

Here was a mystery to be sure! However, I caressed briefly between the trim, saucy little cheeks of her arse and then went to work with the whipcord. No harem whipping would ever lodge in her memory vividly than this, I swore. Her slim neck and the fine blond hair upswept to her top-knot twisted urgently from side to side. The woven cord whipped—and whipped—and whipped—across the taut little rounds of Julie's bottom-cheeks, sometimes catching the inner edges.

Why had the sulky little face with its vacant mouth, petulant air, and whining manner asked for this? The plum-coloured tracery of lash marks soon embroidered Julie's fair-skinned little seat-cheeks and there were such forlorn cries and desperate squirming. Yet the cries were not as shrill or frantic as one might expect. It was then that I noticed what the little tart was doing. She had the edge of the stool between her thighs and was frigging herself between the legs upon it! Though it did not, of course, enter her cunt, she was able to squeeze her clitoris upon it and rub it between her love-lips. No doubt she had learnt such tricks from Maggie!

All my scruples were now overcome. I cracked the cord across Julie's pert backside a dozen more times, and then a dozen again. Towards the end, she gave a short, aching cry of longing and then with a shuddering and limpness underwent her orgasm before my very eyes.

I hardly expected her to return next night—for what more was there to do? Yet she appeared with an armoury of shiny, black straps and a gag which would fill her mouth full enough to silence all shrillness. Her wish was to be strapped down and gagged. Then I was to thread my way into her love-nest. Next, I was to sodomise her bottom! And, finally, I was to whip her bottom as I had done the night before. Prior to the act of sodomy, there were tubes and nozzles to be inserted in Julie's bottom and vagina so that she might be subjected to the ordeals of enema and douche.

Next day, the inspector revealed to me the secret of her strange conduct. "Why, Mr. Charles," said he, "it is the same on every voyage. I choose the two girls who would most delight the Captain and the owner of the vessel, but who are cool towards those gentlemen. In this case, I confided to Julie that the Captain had been taken by an uncontrollable lust for her. And I put on a long face."

"How so?" I asked.

"I whispered to her that the Captain suffered a grave affliction, a penis of such magnitude and weight that in ordinary business he must keep it strapped to the inside of his leg. Alas, I said, a girl of her slimness and petite figure would be split in two by it. A few nights at most and then we should attend her funeral, the cruelly rendered corpse of beauty tipped over the rail to feed the sharks. I added that her only escape from the Captain was to seek protection in your bed as the ship's owner."

"And yet the range of her perversities?"

"I added, sir, that you were a man who could not endure the same form of pleasure twice in a week with any girl. Unless she could devise variety, you would be sure to send her away."

I could not but chuckle at the ingenious fellow, for Julie was just stupid enough to believe such a tale.

"And the Captain?" I asked.

"Well, Mr. Charles," said he, "I separately informed Noreen that she was in the gravest danger: you had conceived a murderous resentment against her for her betrayal of you. Now that you were absolute master, a dreadful fate lay in store for her: you would have her brought to your cabin, and there two monstrous Arab emissaries would use her day and night, rending her cunt and sodomising her bottom with grievous results. The lash would also be applied pitilessly to her backside. After two days and two nights, the more brutal of the two emissaries would take a stout cord, tighten it slowly 'round her throat, and her lifeless corpse would be pushed out through the porthole."

"How readily you malign me!" I said, smiling.

"Indeed, sir. I informed Noreen that her last hope was to seek refuge in the Captain's bed and never emerge from his cabin. Whatever his demands—however extreme—she must comply with them to the letter or else be turned away and fall victim to your revenge."

We laughed heartily over this and then parted. To tell the truth, I sought a respite from Julie's advances and had just decided to appoint Maggie as my cabin-girl. That night, however, there was a terrible outcry and sounds of a struggle. I heard a shout that the

Captain's arm had been broken, and then another voice adding that Noreen had done it deliberately. It seemed at first to contradict the very basis of the inspector's plan. Yet, as luck would have it, Noreen had been lurking nearby and had heard every word of his explanation to me! Furious at what she had submitted to without need, she had revenged herself violently upon the captain of the *Brandon*.

Here was a pretty pickle! The ship was in no danger, but it was clear that we could not permit mutiny to go unpunished. The Captain claimed his right to mete out retribution. With his right arm bound up, this seemed absurd. Yet he confided to us that he wished merely to give Noreen a stern lecture.

Knowing Noreen, we could not approve the leniency—or its wisdom. Yet the Captain was her victim and, as such, privileged to choose. Next day, on the eve of which she was to be scolded, the firmly built, nineteen-year-old trollop showed no remorse. Her first duty was to swab the deck on all fours with bucket and cloth. The Captain looked on. How tight the jeans strained over the strapping young cheeks of Noreen's bottom! Sensing his presence, she sat back. With a shake of her fringe, she stared with all the insolence her pale features and brown eyes could express. There was so sign of repentance whatever.

That evening, our two stewards, Karim and Saleh, escorted her to the Captain's cabin. The poor fellow sat on a comfortable chair and chose to have Noreen strapped face down over his lap for the scolding. For safety's sake, they pinioned her securely so that she could hardly twitch a muscle. The Captain looked down and saw the two cheeks of Noreen's arse, tightly sheathed in denim, facing up towards him. Down came the jeans, and the conversation turned to the subject of Noreen's knickers!

Noreen's knickers were, it seemed, of the tightest, briefest cotton. The Captain expressed interest at such tight, scanty encasing of the sturdy, full-cheeked backside of a strapping young trollop, as he habitually termed her. Noreen's knickers came down too. It was, of course, necessary to prevent her answering back during the scolding. The still warm cottom, carefully folded and secured, made an admirable bridle.

Now he was alone with her. We listened intently. A match flared and the Captain drew gently at a rich Havana. "I shall scold you now, Noreen, for quite half an hour. Ah, there is nothing like a choice cheroot for bringing the roses to a pair of pale cheeks! Keep that backside of yours quite still, if you please! Why, I vow you would break your straps if they were any less stout than they are! Such determination, Noreen!"

It seemed the ship's cat must be trapped in there somewhere. Surely it was a shrill feline mewing which obscured some of the Captain's words, as we clustered outside the door to listen! He seemed to smile as he spoke, as if his injury had become amusing to him.

"Your first taste of ordeal by a glowing cheroot, Noreen? Ah, those strapping, nineteen-year-old bottom-cheeks of yours! How many men have admired them in tight denim, as you worked on all fours at your polishing! Did you reward their admiration by a flick of your dark fringe and a cold stare? Then how those gentlemen would love to be in my place now!"

There came the dry squeak of leather strained in vain.

"An ardent caress on the crown of your left-hand arse-cheek to begin, Noreen! Ah, does that make your toes curl? You would burst our eardrums were it not for the wadding! A moment to draw the Havana to brightness. Now we can rouge you as daringly as we like on your arse-cheeks, Noreen, since they are not the ones you display to the world!"

The feline mewing made his next remark inaudible. Then we heard his voice once more.

"A moment to brush away the grey blemish of ash, Noreen! And now the ardent red touched to your pale bottom-cheek once more. . . . Ah, what a soprano aria you would sing if you could, Noreen! . . So deep a blush already. . . . Do you try to turn the other cheek in order to spare this one? So desperate already, Noreen, to feel the vital glow on the other side? Have no fear, its turn shall come. First, let us tap the ash and draw. A little more touching-up on this cheek first. We must rouge it quite outrageously!"

His words were lost to us for a moment. Then he said presently, "Dare we highlight the dark valley between the snow hills, Noreen? Let us be bold! The red glow marks our trace along that rear valley's lower slope. I hear a zephyr blow rudely, do I not? Such high notes, Noreen. An encore is imperative! Now we ascend the second bottom-hill, as yet so pale. . . . Those stout, leather straps will not break, Noreen. Resign yourself to that! A fall of powdered grey and now the touch of ardent cherry red. Such is the penalty of violence, Noreen! After this you shall be my obedient cabin-girl!"

So it proved, showing the power of scolding over a trollop!

Tomorrow we sight land, they say. Every hour brings closer

Your own adoring Charlie

Port Rif, 1 August 1904

My dearest Lizzie,

As a POSTSCRIPT to my epistle written on board ship, I send this briefest of notes to tell you that I am now safely arrived on the continent which holds within it your own sweet self! How long it will be before I see you again, I dare not say. It may be many weeks or, by a happy chance, I may overtake this very letter with the wings of adoration! It depends much on the disposal of my "cargo" and the state of my late Uncle Brandon's affairs here.

I will, however, regale you a moment with the events of the last night of our voyage. The inspector, who has now quite deserted his post in England for some more lucrative employment here among the traders, continued in his role of master of ceremonies. He devised what he promised would be a Rabelesian banquet for our final dinner: the best food, the finest vintages, and a bevy of nude damsels to attend to our every desire! You may well believe that not one of his invitations was declined! The result was both inexpressibly randy and yet comic at the same time.

We entered the main saloon with its silks and cut glass. I vow, Lizzie, I experienced a combination of sensations unknown to me before: a stiffening penis and a desire to roar with laughter. Separately, these are common enough. Together, they must be rare indeed.

Ahead of me was the banquet table at which the inspector, the Captain, and I were to sit. It consisted of a light, wooden surface, some six feet long and two feet across, and a hole cut in the middle through which the lighting column rose. What is so curious, then, you ask? The table was supported at either end, not by legs but on the backs of two figures kneeling on all fours. Well, you say, such carvings are not unusual. Ah, but these were not carved figures. The nude flesh of Maggie and Noreen was more succulently moulded! The stools over which they were strapped supported them in turn and the tabletop was secured by a harness 'round their waists and shoulders. A man who sat on one side would have Maggie's blond head protruding on his left-hand side, from under the table end, and the pale spread of Noreen's strapping young hips on his right. Those who sat opposite would have Noreen's face and Maggie's rump either side of their chairs!

The lighting was more ingenious still. Our good inspector had had cause to arrest three loud-mouthed street girls, some fourteen years old, for their noisy conduct. He had carefully ensured that they should be among our cargo in order that he might have some stock to drive to market.

Mandy, Tracy, and Sal (as Sally preferred to be known) stood naked upon the central platform of the table and provided our candelabra. Their wrists were joined in the leather cuffs above. It was Sal who provided the light for me and to whom I gave the most attention. What a pint-sized little strumpet she was at thirteen or fourteen! Imagine a broad, highboned face with rouge on the cheeks. Picture the snub little nose and the dark, defiant eyes. Add to it a collar-length crop of fair, tousled, wavy hair. In her figure, she was not tall, even for her age. Unlike the elegance of Tracy's skirts, Sal's costume for roaming the streets included the tight denim of her working trousers. Picture the two as they must have been—almost like boy and girl!—the firm tomboy thighs and the fat little cheeks of Sal's bottom rolling as she walked, filling the tight jeans cloth so heavily!

Now, like her two young friends, she posed naked on the pedestal. Like them, too, she had an ingenious dildo threaded in her cunt, curving out in the front to become a triple candle holder with its three tall flames twelve inches or so from her belly. At the rear, an identical candelabrum had been firmly inserted between the fat little cheeks of her arse!

Vanessa and the other girls attended as our charming naked waitresses. As we awaited the first course, the inspector told us humorously of his arrest of the three street girls. How they had gone through the quiet middle-class thoroughfares, Sal bawling her war song: "I go out on Saturday night, and I look for a fucking fight!" How she had insolently begged for a cigarette—"Got any fags?"—and how she had surrendered to the riff-raff melting pot of society. Having apprehended the three young strumpets, he was struck at once by the thought of being a partner in Uncle Brandon's business rather than a mere assistant.

Six waitresses entered, almost staggering under the weight of the huge salver, whose cover still hid from us our banquet. The splendid piece was loaded onto the table and the cover removed. Can you guess, my sweet?

It was twenty-five-year-old Jackie, the promiscuous young slut with her bell of blond hair, impudent blue eyes, sullen jaw, and fattish hips. Have no fear, she was not the meal itself, merely the delectable platter. Upon her breasts were arranged the hors d'oeuvres, so that her nipples appeared as the cherries atop them, for she was entirely naked. Jackie's sluttish young body was to provide all the plate and glass we required. We took wine by pouring it into her mouth and she turned her blond head obediently to the imbiber and gave him the draught from her mouth into his, nicely mulled.

Our fingers worked eagerly on the salad of the hors d'oeuvres, the slightly acid tingling of the salad dressing causing Jackie's nipples to stiffen remarkably. Finger bowls were not needed: glancing down at the firm, pale insolence of Noreen's face, I had only to hold my fingers to her mouth and command her tongue to do the work. There were some very firm bananas in the fruit bowl and you will believe I could resist taking one in my other hand. Maggie's blond hair, as well as her crude, pale features, were reflected for me in a mirror. As I coaxed the banana into Mag's young cunt, she was as eager as I. Then her tongue washed the Captain's fingers lovingly.

Was Noreen more or less fortunate? In her case, the inspector took a different aim. The banana entered between the pale, strapping cheeks of Noreen's nineteen-year-old bottom. That left only one receptacle for the olive stones of the salad. In my own case—for I enjoy a meal of olives—I judged it uncouth to litter floor and table. To recompense my young blonde, with her firmly broadened buttocks and thighs, I first gave her a frig-jig with the banana. Then, one by one, I popped the olive stones up her arse-hole. We now went on to the salmon mayonnaise and asparagus.

The main dish was served upon the proud curve of Jackie's young belly, though the asparagus stalks were tucked deeply into her love-pouch, protruding between her thighs, which gave them a most novel savour. We ate heartily, but did not forget the hunger of those who supported us. In my case, it was possible only to feed Noreen from my hand. She hesitated at first but the folly of refusing such delicious morsels was soon shown her. In the end, she ate with relish some of the asparagus impregnated with Jackie's own girl taste.

I will not weary you with every course and wine we enjoyed. The dessert was of pancakes, and for this we required a clean platter. It required only Jackie to turn over on her mayonnaised belly in order for the pancakes to be served upon her seat-cheeks. They were hot enough to make her stir a little but not excessively so. The advantage of the pale, fattish cheeks of Jackie's arse was that they provided a convenient central cleavage for the droplets of lemon and sugar. To dunk each bit of pancake between Jackie's sluttish bum-cheeks was most lewdly enjoyable.

Our banquet ended with fruit of the season: grapes accompanied by peaches and plums. Jackie would take the grapes in her mouth, pop them open, remove the pips with her tongue, then feed the fruit into the mouth of the man whose open lips covered hers. Plums she treated similarly but, turning her head, Jackie was of course obliged to spit the stone lightly into the man's hand. Maggie shook her blond fringe indifferently, but there was some apprehension in her blue-green eyes. A plum stone, after all, is a size larger than that of an olive. Alas for Maggie! How easy it is to eat those sweet, syrupy plums voraciously. I thought of those men who had pressed at the Greystones stable window to goggle at the young blond saddle-dresser as she worked with her nonchalant sluttishness in tight riding jeans. Imagine their delight now, had they been able to see the intruding banana, the waste bowl presented to Maggie's bottom, and the slow, measured clatter of falling plum and olive stones.

I thought how inexpressibly randy and delicious it was to have one's dinner impregnated by the skin flavours of a girl's most intimate body surfaces. We pushed back our chairs a little and lit our cheroots. This was charmingly done: it was young Sal who was my human candelabrum. Once I had the weed between my teeth, she backed a little towards me and bent over so that the rear triple candle was presented. She had to tuck her knees forward a little, for Sal, of course, stood above me. You may be sure I detained her a moment in this posture.

When the meal was over, the inspector begged our indulgence. He would take his three young street girls to another saloon, for an Arab harem buyer was coming out in his barge this evening, with a view to purchasing all three for his collection. You may be sure that the Captain and I took up positions outside the door, listening and endeavouring to catch keyhole glimpses.

With an eye to a good profit, the inspector once again dressed Sally as a young slut of the streets, in her black, waist-length jerkin and the tight, pale-blue denim of her working trousers. The harem owner murmured approvingly. He said he liked young hoydens of fourteen or so who challenged him by disobedience. Such ill-bred defiance was plain in Sal's broad and high-boned face, dark eyes, and shock of fair hair. He spoke eagerly of sturdy little hips and firm thighs. Had she been trained by sport and exercise?

Perhaps she struggled a little as the two valets held her by either arm and his hand ran under the gusset of jeans cloth. Was Sal a virgin? The inspector could not claim that, but he hastily assured the harem master that it had only been boys of Sal's own age. In the passageways of the town, Sal would also suck the penis of older men in exchange for cigarettes.

The harem buyer did not seem unduly displeased to learn of her experience in such a craft. Seduced by the swagger of Sal's fat little bottom as she walked, he required the valets next to turn and bend the young strumpet. He inquired if the virginity of Sal's young arse had been taken. The inspector vouched it had not. The harem buyer thus became master of all three girls and was left alone with them, assisted by the two valets.

"Away with your skirts and pants, my three houris! Excellent! Mandy—on the bed and make love to yourself! Tracy—join her! Sally, bottom upwards over the pillows, if you please. Why, the top of your head scarcely reaches a man's shoulder, and yet how many you have made to lust after you, Sal, as you walked through the streets, rolling your fat little bottom-cheeks in working jeans!"

At his command the valets tightened the wrist straps on his young mistress. "How often have you made respectable husbands follow you, Sally? How often have cameras clicked upon your face and your rear view to add gems to their private collections? Why, you even intrude into the marriage bed, I dare-

say! As they do their duty to their wives, their minds
are elsewhere. They dream of taking you down to the
county wine vaults or the monks' rendezvous in the
old churchyard. They dream of such fucking, even of
buggering Sal's fat little bottom at thirteen or fourteen
years old!"

There was a pause and then he continued more
breathlessly. "Absurd to refuse me your rear virginity, Sally! Your attempt merely earns you a reprimand afterwards! Were you so haughty with the yo-
kel boys who kept your company in the merchant's
passage? Bite the pillow, Sally, to give you greater
endurance! Ah, how copiously I shall spend my seed
on this hot, infertile soil!" Ten minutes later, his furious cries confirmed that he had pumped his lust
into Sal's backside, where no unwanted progeny is
engendered.

"Now, Sally," he murmured, "there is one other
joy which the men who admired you in the streets
would have relished. It requires this whip with the
lash of woven snakeskin. Karim, my fine fellow!
Teach the young slut a lesson! Let me see the
cheeks of Sal's bottom resemble a pair of skinned
tomatoes!"

The sounds that rose from Sally, though a vulgar
young strumpet, can well be imagined. As it happened, I had a rendezvous with Maggie in my own
cabin just then. It was the last before she, too, was
sold to the highest bidder at the auction block. The
Captain and the inspector, however, were privileged
to spy through the crack of the door where Sally
sprawled on her belly over the divan.

There were many worthy citizens of the elegant
city who would have wished such a loud-mouthed
young slut punished. Karim did not disappoint them,
I was assured. By the time he had visited the fat,

squirming little cheeks of Sal's bottom with his lash, she could not have endured sitting on the lightest feather cushion without a cry! The Captain and the inspector watched, mouths open with amazement and delight at Sally's shrill descant. There was much satisfaction that such a master should have purchased her.

Thus we came safe ashore this morning, my dearest Lizzie. I was not sorry to part with the Captain and the inspector, for their vindictiveness towards the rebels among the girls suits ill my own more softly lascivious tastes. However, who can say that young Sally did not need some whipping of the kind? As for Noreen, I had no compunction over the "scolding" which the Captain, with his leisurely Havana, had administered to her strapping young seat!

In a day or two the last of our business will be done. Events make it impossible that I should return to England, even were I so inclined. All my thoughts now turn towards you. Be sure, my love, that the final journey between us shall be accomplished with the minimum of delay by your own adoring

Charlie

My very own Charles,

I WRITE AT once to tell you of a most remarkable spectacle, which is continuing even as I pen these words. It is an "experimental lecture," performed on the person of an attractive young Englishwoman, in front of an invited audience. Dr. Jacobus, a crony of the Pasha, is to demonstrate the sexual anatomy and functions of this young wife.

Two days ago the Pasha mentioned it to me. An examination table was to be set out under bright lights on a dais in the walled courtyard. Twenty of his friends, connoisseurs of the female body and owners of private harems, would dine with him. After dinner they would adjourn to the outdoor "lecture theatre," where the learned Dr. Jacobus would illustrate every form of sexual enjoyment which the young woman could offer. It was expected that the lecture would continue long after midnight.

"But, surely," I objected, "no woman would consent unless she were a slave and was given no choice? Yet, if she were a slave, her master would scarcely abandon her to such a purpose?"

"True," smiled the Pasha, "however, in Lesley's case, she has just lost her freedom but has not yet been sold by the trader. She is thus the ideal subject for the good Dr. Jacobus."

My curiosity was afire! I was determined, if possible, to be one of the learned audience at the experimental lecture! It was, for obvious reasons, confined to men of great trust who would not regret anything that Lesley might undergo.

How well our cunning Pasha guessed my intention, Charlie! I slipped into the courtyard while they were at dinner and inspected the arrangements. The large marble table was on the dais, a cupboard of accessories standing behind it. The seats rose slightly in three tiers, curved to give each occupant a perfect view, no more than ten feet from the demonstration table. To speak the truth, my dearest, they were more old-fashioned sedan chairs than seats, each having tall, curtained sides so that no spectator could see another. During her ordeal, of course, Lesley would be able to see them all. Why such privacy? In each booth was a girl to minister to the occupant's needs as the lecture provoked them.

Mathematics was never your strong point, my beloved. Yet think. Twenty spectators and twenty-*one* seats! Were I seen at this demonstration, what a scandal there must be! So, our thoughtful Pasha had provided an extra place for my concealment. I moved to the empty booth at the end of the first row and took my perch.

Who was the slave girl in the next seat? I could not help furtively peeking through the curtaining enough to peep. Behold, it was Patrizia, the eighteen-year-old Italian bride. She is short and sturdy as a tomboy of sixteen, dark-brown hair worn straight to her collar and parted on her forehead, like a medieval page. Such olive-skinned appeal, wide cheekbones under dark eyes, and a firm line to mouth and jaw!

Now the Pasha and his guests came out into the courtyard, he directing them away from the booth which concealed me. "That is set aside, gentlemen! The rest are at your disposal!"

Smiling at his cunning, I peeped into the next booth. A fair-skinned man of fifty or so with silvered hair and moustaches was the guest. Patrizia stood before him in a blue blouse and matching drawers, skin-tight from waist to knees, worn with a belt of pale-brown leather. Still such a playful but innocent girl, her eyes widened with astonishment when he made her sit on his knee and kiss him. Unbuttoning her blouse, he moulded her full, Italian breasts with his hands. Then, standing her up, he admired her firm, though somewhat stocky, thighs. He turned her 'round. From the rear, her hips sloped downward and outward, giving her a delightful, broad-bottomed tomboy look. Though not fat in the seat, her rear-cheeks have a voluptuous weight. The tight pants' crease behind her knees and across the back of her thighs. Deeper folds curve from between her legs under the full, olive-skinned cheeks of Patrizia Luisi's bottom.

The murmur of voices fell silent as Dr. Jacobus came onto the dais, where the lights shone bright as noon. He was a very smartly dressed man of Latin appearance. About forty-five years old, he seemed the dark-haired medical scholar, with knowing eyes.

"This evening, gentlemen, we are fortunate in our subject," said he, sharing the amusement of his listeners. "Lesley is a young, married woman, twenty-eight years old. Until recently, she led a life of promiscuous sexual emancipation. You need have no compunction, then, over what is done to her here. She is well used to the penis, both in marriage and outside it, being willful and selfish in her lusts. Moreover, child-rearing has given her a firmly controlled maturity of figure, enabling her to bear far more than could be inflicted on a schoolgirl of fourteen or fifteen."

The learned doctor glanced 'round at us and continued. "Lesley is an educated young wife, emancipated and self-possessed. Yet her arrogant and disdainful manner makes her a more exciting challenge. How remorselessly we shall pursue extreme possibilities in dealing with her lips, her breasts, her vagina, and her backside!" He lowered his voice confidentially. "Some of the ordeals which Lesley will presently undergo would be frankly impossible if she were still free and able to tell tales. Fortunately, she is already destined for a life of sexual slavery in a place from which no complaints are ever heard. When Lesley lived freely with husband and lovers, the mere unwanted display of a stranger's penis to her was an offence! The use of it on her without her grudging consent was a crime! The whip across her bare bottom was deemed torture! Happily, such words are meaningless here, where her master's pleasure is the law."

Two of the Pasha's soldiers brought her on to the dais. How shall I describe the young woman? Lesley is quite tall and, at twenty-eight years old, her body is kept nicely trim. Her straight, fair hair is cropped almost boyishly short at the nape, shaped close to her head from its high crown to her jaw line, and parted in a long fringe on her forehead. Aloof blue eyes are matched by firm, fair-skinned features, with a sulky downward turn of mouth and sullen chin. She is a girl of English good looks, well bred, but spoilt by her moody expression. How her figure would thrill you! She wore only a white singlet and a pair of translucent stocking-tights in honey-toned silk. Dr. Jacobus pulled up the singlet front to her throat, revealing the milk-white hillocks of Lesley's breasts, with their pink cherry tips. His demonstration cane stroked the two flesh mounds.

"Let us begin, gentlemen, with Lesley's breasts. Ah, see how she lowers her eyes until her fringe hides them! Are you shy about showing your tits, Lesley? Observe the admirable elasticity, gentlemen, despite having given suck to a pair of infants. As I lay the cane underneath and lift them, see how proudly they keep their shape!"

The young woman bowed her urchin crop farther.

"Don't close your eyes, Lesley!" smiled Dr. Jacobus. "Watch how your tits move when the cane raises them. Now, gentlemen, be assured that Lesley's nipples are no different than those of the finest duchess or the lowest whore. However great her repugnance for being publicly displayed like this, she cannot help her little cherries growing hard when they are caressed. We need not even use our fingers! Watch the metal tip of the lecture cane!"

He circled the cool metal lightly on the young wife's left nipple, which seemed to pop up at once. Then the right one came next. A soldier held Lesley's head up to face the audience, while Jacobus bent and tongue-flicker each nipple in turn.

Now his cane traced the slight proud outward curve of her belly. "A modern young woman! Bicycle exercise and healthy activity! A belly swell or two from her babies has not runied her here." The cane travelled down farther. How suggestively the transparent gloss of tights moulds her lower half! How trim and almost boyish her long thighs are!

Higher up, the fair pubic hair, pressed by the tights, shows through like pretty fern. The firm pubic mound and the beginning of the cleft between her vaginal lips appear admirably!"

He nodded to the two soldiers, who turned her so we now enjoyed her rear view. Lesley stood with her head bowed again, the short fair hair parting under its own weight on the back of her neck.

"How fortunate," said our lecturer, "that Lesley was made to have babies. Child-rearing has merely imparted a gentle maturity of hips, a slight firming-out to the cheeks of Lesley's bottom. The transparent film of honey-coloured tights is like her seventh veil, showing the pale swell of Lesley's bottom-moons and the dusky forbidden cleavage between them."

He traced the cane over the contours of her derrière. Lesley's hind-cheeks tightened in alarm at the playful menace of bamboo. "That frightens her a little," said Jacobus. "Lesley knows that, when her tights are taken down, she will be spared nothing. The thought that her bare arse will be caned as pitilessly as in any prison makes her knees and bowels tremble. Try to calm yourself, Lesley. It will not be for some hours yet."

There was no mistaking her tension. How her knees pressed hard together and her seat-cheeks contracted as Dr. Jacobus went on! "If child-bearing has made her vagina a little slacker, it has given her a behind like a young Spartan soldier-girl. For those whose penis shafts prefer tightness, it offers the exquisite grip of Lesley's anus. She must learn to ask her lovers for that!"

Lesley looked 'round over her shoulder with a start. How wide were those blue eyes under the parted fringe of her urchin crop!

"There need be no compunction," said Dr. Jacobus, smiling at her. "For too long Lesley has indulged her own pleasures at the expense of others. She can hardly complain now if she is made to submit to the demands made upon her!"

He made her bend over, and the tights shaped the broadened swell of her bum-cheeks, tautly rounded. Imagine her in some black trouser suit, like a coolie, bending right over to weed the garden. No doubt the sight of Lesley's arse fully spread would cause many a penis to stiffen, many a furtive camera to click for a set of pictures for a private collection. But that was nothing to the view she offered reluctantly to the audience here.

The lecture began in earnest with Lesley's mouth. Dr. Jacobus traced its sulky line with his finger. He ordered her to kiss his fingertips and then the back of his hand, as he stroked her lips. When she hesitated, he whispered a warning in her ear. Lesley forlornly pouted her lips, kissing his fingers and knuckles with alarmed eagerness. He slid three fingers into her mouth and required her to wash them with her tongue.

Next she was obliged to demonstrate the art of kissing with the first of the Pasha's soldiers. In the first bout of passion, as she pressed her closed lips against his, the Arab soldier tried to bruise her with his force. At last he bit her lower lip until she yielded a muffled cry.

"You must open your lips, Lesley!" said Dr. Jacobus, laughing. "Intrude your tongue into his mouth and let him taste your saliva. Show your enthusiasm, unless you wish to see your young nymph whipped. The learned scholars at this lecture would be greatly intrigued by a schoolgirl daughter, thirteen years old!"

Into the Arab's mouth Lesley's tongue fluttered wildly like a trapped butterfly. At last the soldier pushed her head back and thrust his own tongue into her mouth. At the same time he made Lesley put her hand upon his hardening erection and unbutton him. The brown-toned penis stood stiff and sinewy. He pushed her to her knees in front of him.

"Lesley's lips are shaped by nature to suck the penis," said Dr. Jacobus. "It will be required several times a day by harem guards. To swallow is not essential, but it is always commanded in such places as a sign of love and submission to the man."

Lesley's fair urchin crop twisted in the hands of the man who stood before her. Another warning brought her to her senses. She bowed her head and took the penis in her hands, peeling back the foreskin with her thumbs, and running her tongue in the sensitive groove under it. The soldier clenched his teeth in a grimace of pleasure as Lesley tongue-tipped the vent of his knob.

"Pay no attention to the pretence of repugnance Lesley showed at first," Jacobus told us. "She fell so in love with the last man whose mistress she was that she did the deed for him several times. If she was prepared to win him by such means, there can be no excuse for her now. She admitted these episodes after her abductors pressed her upon the subject. True, she has never swallowed before, but that is merely a gesture of obedience."

The soldier guided Lesley's mouth up and down the penis shaft, his hands pressing on her short-cut fair hair. Once or twice we heard the young wife retch faintly.

"Ah," said Jacobus, "the knob drives close to the back of her throat—or else she tastes the man's lubrication in her saliva!"

The soldier required Lesley to suck faster and faster, so that one guessed the outcome. He gave a cry in his fury and shot the first warm spawn onto the young wife's tongue.

"Swallow properly," said Dr. Jacobus gently, "or else bear the consequences, Lesley. Good. Now, wash the knob with your tongue."

We saw the movements in her rounded mouth, her tongue working softly 'round the penis she had just fed from. In drawing away, the man bestowed a final trail upon her mouth's upper rim.

"Lick your lips, Lesley," said Dr. Jacobus, and she obeyed.

At this moment I could not resist peeping into my neighbour's booth. Patrizia sat on her heels before the worthy gentleman. Her olive-skinned face, with its broad high cheekbones, was almost hidden in his lap, the dark-brown hair across her forehead touching his belly. Yet I saw Patrizia's mouth rounded as she sucked his tool.

"Close your eyes, Patrizia!" he breathed softly. "Imagine it is a month ago—your honeymoon. Pretend it is your young bridegroom you suck!"

On the dais, Lesley was still standing before the marble-topped table.

"Lie on the demonstration-table, Lesley!" said Dr. Jacobus sharply.

Turning her back, she lodged one knee on the rim to climb up. As she went forward on her hands, the tights presented the seat of our trim young Amazon in a most provocative posture. It was this which earned from Dr. Jacobus a well-aimed smack on Lesley's rear-cheeks. She gasped, spreading one hand back over her rump as she completed her ascent.

"Lie on your back," said he, "your feet towards us. Now hug your knees up to your breasts."

She did as she was told. The young woman was now presented to us with her hips and arse in a full squat, seen from underneath. Dr. Jacobus placed two rubber cushions under her head so that her face was visible at the same time. I wondered why she was not yet undressed completely, though the transparent film of the tights perfectly outlined every detail of her love-slit in this present posture.

"Lesley's vagina will be the centre of interest for many of her admirers," said Dr. Jacobus, smiling. "Let us study its main features. Towards her belly, where the tip of the demonstration cane is touching her, stands her clitoris, not quite masked by her fair pubic hair. If we were to require Lesley to masturbate in front of us that is where she would probably begin to rub herself. See how sensitive she is even to the metal tip of the pointer through her tights. Of all her playthings, Lesley's clitoris is the one she would die rather than part with."

He drew the tip farther back. "Here you will see the main outline of her vulva, that purse of flesh which represents its outer lips. The entrance to her vagina now appears as a mere pink slit—just there. Remember, though, that it can be stretched to take the largest penis and must even permit the emergence of a baby's body. Not far away, we have a smaller hole from which a golden fountain plays several times a day."

He now sat on the table's edge, laid down the lecture cane, and traced her anatomy with his fingers. "Lesley no doubt believes in her right to masturbate if she chooses. Some harem philosophies deny that, in order to ensure that she does not spoil herself for her master. In that case, she must be circumcised, as it is called, secured in this posture for that purpose. An older and experienced harem woman will use a keen little blade to prune away Lesley's clitoris and trim her vaginal lips well back. They will leave her nothing to play with. After that, her pleasure will be concentrated on the use of the man's penis in her vagina or, if preferred, her behind. The chosen area will be prepared by constant stimulus and excitation from the women who have charge of her."

As he spoke, he rubbed Lesley's clitoris lightly in a teasing circular movement with his fingertips. We could hear the young wife breathing harder, the whisper of stockinged knees and thighs pressing and squirming together. With the index finger of his other hand, Dr. Jacobus simultaneously parted her vaginal lips in a long, repeated caress. Lesley's mouth opened a little, her eyes closed, fluttered open, and then closed again.

"More probably," said Dr. Jacobus, "she will be encouraged to play with herself, even before her master and his guests, as well as to indulge in amours with other harem girls."

She turned her fair urchin crop aside, as if needing to rest her head on her shoulder. Her tongue passed repeatedly and automatically over her parted lips.

"You do like it, don't you, Lesley?" He smiled gently, then addressed himself to the rest of us. "Now, gentlemen, what better way to gauge her passion than to see how her love juice collects on the silk of her tights? She cannot help herself. It is immaterial whether the hand is that of her lover or of a man she despises and loathes."

He spoke truly. The honey-toned sheen of the tights now shone with the slippery wetness of her vaginal lubrication which gathered on the mesh between her legs. Dr. Jacobus cupped his hand over her vagina, squeezing and milking gently. Lesley gave an imploring little cry. Was she frantic not to be brought to orgasm in front of us? Or was she begging him to help her scale the heights of bliss? Alas, Dr. Jacobus drew his hand away. He locked a thin chain round her waist and clipped it to a metal ring at the table's centre, restricting her to the tabletop. "Turn on your side, Lesley," he said gently, "and draw your knees up. I'm going to peel your tights down to mid-thigh."

When this was done, he turned to us. "Even a man whom she dislikes can conquer Lesley if he is prepared to masturbate her to a point where she is beyond self-control. Even an educated and self-possessed young woman will yearn for a body to respond to. There will come a point where she will want sex with any man who is available, or even with another woman. Watch carefully while I continue to masturbate Lesley between the rear opening of her legs."

On to the dais came a quite tall and graceful Caribbean beauty. I saw it was Shawn, in a yellow singlet and beige shorts. Such a proud, high-boned facial beauty. Her dark hair was once more prettily drawn back in a bun. Her bare coffee-skinned legs were long and agile. As she stripped off her pants, the tawny cheeks of her bottom were elegantly rounded, her pubic mound bearing a trim bush of dark hair.

As Dr. Jacobus continued to masturbate Lesley by rubbing his finger in her vaginal slit, Shawn stooped and tauntingly put her eighteen-year-old lips to those of the lust-tormented wife. Lesley kissed yearningly, giving a little whimper of frustration when Shawn drew away. The tawny-skinned girl gave a secret smile from her almond eyes and gathered saliva on her tongue. Lesley, her hips moving in time with Dr. Jacobus' stroking, opened her mouth pleadingly to take the coloured girl's well-watered tongue on her own. Shawn stooped right over the young English-woman and, pulling up her singlet, offered her warm toned young breasts. Lesley took the nipple crowns one after the other in her mouth, eyes closed in rapture, and tongue-washed them languorously. Dr. Jacobus' fingers, entering through the rear open-ing of her thighs, now fondled her clitoris pitilessly.

Of course Shawn was a warm-blooded girl who was herself getting very excited by now. She lay on the table, facing Lesley but with her head towards Lesley's feet. Shawn's tawny thighs now opened in front of Lesley's face. With hardly a moment of hesi-tation, the urchin-cropped wife began to kiss the tops of the long, graceful Caribbean legs. Shawn looked down, tight-lidded almond eyes full of mockery, the dark hair with its top-knot and tortoise-shell comb giving her a commanding elegance.

"Do it with your tongue between Shawn's legs," said Dr. Jacobus quietly. Then he turned to us. "An intriguing tableau, gentlemen! Lesley swears she has never made love with a young woman before, not even her girlfriends at school or college! Yet nature has taught her by instinct what to do. Even her mar-riage and babies have not spoilt that."

We stared wide-eyed at the scene on the demon-stration table. Lesley was still restricted to the length of her waist chain. The high crown of her short crop bowed forward. Shawn bent one knee and raised her leg a little. Lesley licked and kissed the brown-skinned girl's clitoris, then lapped at Shawn's vaginal cleft as if the elixir of life ran from between her cunt-lips. The firm, pale moons of Lesley's bottom seemed to arch out at the same time towards Dr. Jacobus, as she lay on her side. From the rear opening of her thighs, he continued to masturbate her with remorseless skill.

Shawn's eyes were closed in a dream of bliss, her cheek resting on Lesley's bare hip, arms hugging the Englishwoman's haunches, and lips caressing.

"Turn over, Shawn," said Dr. Jacobus presently, "show your behind to Lesley. Reach back and pull the cheeks apart a little."

The high, taut, coffee-skinned cheeks of Shawn's bottom were delectable enough. Yet Lesley twisted her face away, lips pressed and mewing with refusal.

"Would you rather a certain little girl did it instead?" asked Dr. Jacobus. "Instructions can be given at once for that."

Lesley, whose reluctance was perhaps half-hearted, looked at him in dismay, then turned her face to Shawn's rump. Cheek-kissing was ordered first, then lipping the dark cleavage, and finally the flickering intrusion of Lesley's tongue into Shawn's tight anus-bud. Yet by this time both girls had liberally dewed the inner surfaces of their thighs with the lubrication of excitement. As Dr. Jacobus had pointed out, it was absurd for Lesley in such a state to pretend that she could not attend to Shawn's posterior before returning to the other girl's vagina once more.

At length, Shawn was led away into the shadows by one of the Pasha's soldiers. It was just possible to see how he stood her against a balustrade, and made her raise her legs and grip his waist, while his penis entered her vigorously from below.

"The culmination of our efforts," said Dr. Jacobus, "in the first hour of the lecture, must be the principal use of Lesley's vagina. That will now be demonstrated to you."

The captain of the guard appeared, his breeches unbuttoned, a fine, stout erection standing out. Without her waist chain being unfastened, Lesley turned onto her back, bending her knees and opening her thighs wide.

"I fear it is greed rather than obedience which makes her so eager now," said Dr. Jacobus. "Yet who would have thought that Lesley, so arrogant and dismissive in her dealings with others when she was at liberty, would be so eagerly promiscuous in bed?"

The captain smiled and knelt on the table between her legs. He found her well prepared by the lecturer's fondling.

"From such frequent use in the marriage bed and in the beds of her lovers, as well as from child-bearing, Lesley's vagina is a trifle slacker than Arab taste generally prefers. Yet that is amply compensated here by the fairness of her skin and the firm agility of her figure."

He spoke truly. Setting his teeth, the captain drove his shaft into Lesley's cunt with a passion which made her catch her breath. Yet she lifted her hips to him and cried out softly with desire. Taking her head between his hands, he kissed her lips. His palm smoothed repeatedly over her proud, young belly. Then his hands went under the singlet and firmed up Lesley's breasts. Lesley drew her knees right up and her white feet seemed to flutter like two pretty birds in her ecstasy. Her eyes closed lightly and, perhaps, she tried to pretend it was her husband or a lover who was doing it ot her. Dr. Jacobus continued his lesson.

"How ill-advised was that society which permitted Lesley to refuse her body to men who admired her but whom she regarded with disdain! Such caprice is not tolerated here in a slave girl. Yet are we not kinder than the world where she was allowed to be so cool and aloof, bestowing her favours grudgingly on husband and lovers alike?"

Lesley arched her back and began to give little cries of "Ah! Ahhh! Ahhhhh!" Her toes clenched tight with joy.

"In the place she is going to," said Dr. Jacobus, "Lesley will be compelled to submit to the penis of whichever master chooses her. No matter if he is hateful or repugnant to her. Despite her self-possesed and emancipated attitudes, she will enjoy his prick just as much. You see her now? You hear her sigh and whimper with love? You observe her firm, white thighs squeezing adoringly on the penis of her man? Yet she could not detest anyone more! He it was, after Lesley's abduction, who also procured her twelve-year-old daughter. Imagine the happy purchaser of two such treasures—consider the possibilities of love and desire, tenderness and chastisement, which such a pair offer him!"

The captain was steadying Lesley's hips now and riding into her with tremendous vigour. She gave a faint, demented scream of pleasure, begging for the warm flood which would calm her fury. "Now!" she cried. "Do it now! Oh, please!"

But the captain, as you may imagine, was intent on prolonging his enjoyment and so paused, in order to begin again.

"You notice that?" said Dr. Jacobus. "Lesley itches for the sperm now. But nature, the supreme arbiter, has arranged matters so that it is her lover who must dictate the time. The precious unction is his, to bestow or withhold as he chooses."

But just then the dam burst, and with a series of short, butting thrusts, the captain pumped his sperm into Lesley's cunt. "Harder you young slut!" he shouted, matching her own rising cries of pleasure. "Your thighs wider! Let me touch your very depths! Again! And again! Now your lips, while I pump you full. Open! Your tongue playing with mine!"

I swear, Charlie, I never imagined such a display could be possible. The effect upon me was indeed stimulating. Imagine how it must affect my neighbour! I peeped through the gap in the curtaining. Patrizia was bent back over the seat and the elderly gentleman was thrusting up vigorously between her thighs, his penis going like a well-oiled piston!

Yet the first part of the lecture was not quite done. "Gentlemen," said Dr. Jacobus, when the captain had buttoned up his trousers and departed, "before we adjourn for a little refreshment, there is one other function of Lesley's vagina which accuracy requires me to mention. It is, of course, the means by which she produces a charming golden stream several times a day. It is rare for scholars of anatomy to see such a young woman performing that act. Happily, we may now remedy the omission. Demands may now be made upon esley which, once more, may now be made upon Lesley which, once more, would have been impossible when she was an emancipated young wife. Being an educated woman, she may even be less shocked by them than an ordinary working girl would be."

Stretched taut, the waist-chain let her lie at the table's edge, on her back, her tights peeled down to mid-thigh.

"Hug your knees up to your breasts again, Lesley," he said quietly. "Now let us see the little fountain play a golden arc onto the grass. Let me feel your belly for a moment. Ah, yes, I'm sure it must be longing to oblige us after the quart of water you were required to drink earlier on."

Did her blue eyes still look aloof? Was her mouth still set in its line of sulky arrogance? I could not say. For now he allowed Lesley to turn her boyishly cropped and parted fringe away from us. His finger tickled a certain dimple in her vaginal pouch, well presented by her horizontal squat. It took her a moment only, for I guessed she was glad of some pretext to enjoy this relief. I saw her bare belly tighten below the hem of her singlet. With a soft, delicate sound, like the gentlest shower drops on a lawn, the glistening arc rose from Lesley's feminine slit in a brief display. She repeated it without further instruction. Our learned Dr. Jacobus stopped her at that point.

"Now pull up your tights, Lesley. You'll lie arse upwards over the table, ready for the next part of the demonstration lecture."

With the edge of her hand, Lesley brushed the parted fringe of her boyish crop clear of her disdainful blue eyes. She drew the transparent silk of the tights up taut over her hips. The waist-chain just allowed her to sit in the shallow channelling at the table edge. Now there occurred an incident to shock polite society, but a matter of light amusement here with a young slave-wife.

Lesley's little fountain proved easier to turn on than to turn off! Her soft entreaty to Dr. Jacobus was too late! Lesley hid her face in her hands at the liquid whispering between her thighs. Sheathed only in filmy tights, she sat in a warm pool of her own making!

Dr. Jacobus had left. The two soldiers, smiling, detained Lesley, sitting in the channelling, until the seat and even the flanks of her tights were well soaked. Then, shortening the waist-chain, they obliged her to lie over the table. Unwilling to meet our eyes, she turned away on her side. We admired the rear of her high-crowned urchin crop, her back's curve in the short singlet, a band of soft, white skin above her hips, the charms of her legs, and her arse in wet tights. The wet seat of the tights clung flawlessly to her rear contours, the light catching a sheen of moisture. Because the soaked film clung so tightly, it revealed her shape yet more completely. It thus gave a fuller and almost fatter look to the cheeks of Lesley's twenty-eight-year-old bottom!

A soldier with a bowl of rose water and a sponge wiped over the table, wringing out the sponge into the bowl. Then, dipping the sponge into the questionable contents, he wiped over the cheeks of Lesley's tights. A curtain fell over the dais. Lesley believed she was in total privacy. Alas, despite appearances, the curtain was translucent, for the light was behind it. We saw her every movement.

Now, Charlie, what do you imagine? Lesley sobbing at having thus disgraced herself? Weeping for the loss of love and marriage? Trembling at whips and punishments? Terrified at the promise of being sold to a master whose cruelties would dew the pillow with her tears each night? How little you know her! She is still that willful and self-indulgent young tart who lived for her own pleasures.

Believe it or not, our trim young Amazon began to play with herself! She did it furtively, for fear of being caught, not daring to peel down her tights. She is an "advanced" young woman, who proclaims her right to explore and enjoy her own body as a way of self-discovery. She will learn here that such acts are forbidden and punished unless carried out on her master's orders.

However, we soon saw the firm moons of Lesley's bottom—for she still lay with her back to us—clenching and swelling rhythmically, wrinkling the wet seat of her tights a little. There rose a silky whisper of stockinged legs squeezing and smoothing together lovingly. Slipping a hand into the front of the waistband and raising one knee a little, she began to rub her clitoris and vaginal slit. All this was mistily visible through the thin silk. For some ten minutes we were able to enjoy watching Lesley masturbate. Her other hand was clenched against her mouth to stifle any sudden cry. A young wife of twenty-eight, well used to her husband's penis and those of her lovers, must pine for them. Lesley had been ridden by the Arab captain, but not to fulfillment. Promiscuous and selfish as she is in her pleasures, our haughty young wife could not resist finishing what had been so well begun!

There was a diverting conclusion to this. After ten minutes or so, Lesley was lubricating herself copiously, the balloon of desire in her loins inflated almost to bursting point. She was strung harder than ever on the rack of passion's torment. A shadow moved behind her as she fiddled hurriedly with herself. The young wife froze into immobility. A hand smacked down hard on the seat of her wet tights with the heavy resonance of silk clinging soaked to cushiony bottom-flesh.

"Stop that at once, Lesley!" said a woman's voice, "this minute!"

How wide with dismay were the blue eyes which

now looked back at us under the long, parted fringe!
She was alarmed at being caught but also at having
brought herself to a worse pitch than ever. Without
resistance, she let her wrists be enclosed in leather
cuffs at the table rim's fastenings. Can you guess the
sequel, Charlie?

Patience! You shall hear all from

Your own adoring Lizzie!

My dear Charlie,

*I*N GREAT HASTE I scribble a few more lines to tell you of Dr. Jacobus' experimental lecture. It has not concluded even as I write, though we are close to midnight!

For a few more minutes behind the curtain, Lesley underwent a sponging at the woman's hands. We were no more than ten or twelve feet from the demonstration table, and there were broad smiles at the sound of her entreaties. Lesley has an importunate voice, like a sulky and willful little girl. She begged whispered for another young woman to finish her. business for her. After an immediate refusal, she whispered for another young owman to finish her. Last, and in vain, she pleaded for a few minutes alone to perform the act which was now so necessary to her peace of mind. The woman laughed softly.

"Forget about such things for tonight, Lesley. Turn over and show me your behind. Ah, yes! I think our guests will find the next hour or two of the lecture most stimulating!"

I report the very words, Charlie, spoken not an

hour since, for in my innocence I had no notion of what to expect. When the curtain was drawn back and Dr. Jacobus stepped forward on the dais again, the scene had changed a little. Lesley was re-attired in tights and singlet, but now she lay face down over a stout leather bolster. Her seat was well raised and broadened by this. Her hands were held at full stretch ahead of her by the wrist cuffs. Leather anklets held her long, trim legs to the opposite rim of the marble demonstration table.

"Gentlemen," said Dr. Jacobus, "we have considered our subject from one view, let us now consider posterior possibilities."

In her present pose, the tantalising film of the tights showed Lesley's seat-cheeks swelling firmly, and marked the dusky cleft between them. Dr. Jacobus drew his lecture cane over these contours, which contracted instinctively at the touch. The learned doctor showed how an active young woman in her middle twenties, her maturity firmly controlled, was often at her best in this area of her charms.

"In Lesley's case," he remarked, "regular penis exercise in the marriage bed and carefully controlled pregnancy has given a taut, proud maturity to her bottom-cheeks without making her in the least flabby."

I could not see the other guests, of course, as Lesley turned her moody, fair-skinned face with a shake of her fringe. Yet, from the sudden look of apprehension in her blue eyes, I believe she must have seen the twenty middle-aged gentlemen looking expectantly at her, each displaying his own interest at the ordeal she was about to undergo.

"In nature," said Dr. Jacobus, "Lesley's bottom has three uses. For a man, the most important is performed by her anus, which is made as a tight and enjoyable entry for the penis. Those who prize such tightness, and those who enjoy spending in a girl's body without fear of engendering a baby, will make good use of her in that way."

At this point one of the scholars interrupted with a question.

"Risks?" said Dr. Jacobus thoughtfully. "When she chose to bear a child, Lesley thereby diminished the tightness of her cunt. Some men who value tightness will now, understandably, demand the use of her anus. Lesley surely has only herself to blame! She was eager for her husband's penis and so became pregnant. Carrying a baby in her belly made her prone to certain trivial afflictions of her rear dimple. Perhaps she remains vulnerable there. Yet that was the cause of her own randiness. Lesley must not expect to deny us our pleasures because of the consequences of hers!"

Dr. Jacobus returned to his theme. "The second purpose of Lesley's backside is to receive chastisement. Scholars through the ages are of one mind that no part of the female anatomy is better suited to this than the buttocks. Since Lesley will never be set at liberty from her fate as a slave girl, we need have no hypocrisy here. She will be chastised by her master on her bare buttocks and the duration of this will be determined solely by his enjoyment."

Lesley pulled vainly at the leather anklets and wrist cuffs with a wail of protest.

"Finally," said Dr. Jacobus, "her behind was made for woman's ease as well as man's pleasure. That subject concerns us only in so far as she may plead her needs as a pretext. It is, of course, a simple matter to deny such a performance or, indeed, to compel it by means of a loaded squirt. Yet she will no doubt try to end a caning or prevent her master's entry by protesting the urgency of her situation. Happily this may be easily checked."

Now he turned to Lesley and took hold of the waistband of her tights. As he drew it down to her knees, the pale hip flesh swelled free a little. Now we looked down on the slight, taut maturity of her pale hips, the gentle firming-out of her bottom-cheeks, and her long, trim thighs. Despite her twenty-eight years and her promiscuous ways, the young wife lowered her face from our sight, for now Dr. Jacobus pressed her two rear moons apart and displayed Lesley's anus. The tight, dark bud shrank from his finger's touch.

"Lesley pleads that she has never had a man that way," he explained. "Alas, she does not realise how greatly that will make the buyers covet her in the slave girl market!"

He stroked Lesley's fair urchin crop as if to calm her. Then he took a glass squirt about eight inches long and slim as a pencil, with a rubber bulb at one end. He filled it from a bottle of liquid soap. Next he sat on the table's edge, firmly circling Lesley's waist with one arm, and looking down at the taut swell of her seat. The skin of the cheeks, where they curved in to meet at her anus, was ivory-yellow, in contrast to the pallor of her buttocks.

The neat inward dimple of Lesley's arse tightened with alarm at the touch of the cold glass squirt. Dr. Jacobus laid the squirt down. With all his power, he delivered a series of ringing smacks upon the full, pale moons of Lesley's bottom. The promiscuous young wife was soon gasping, tensing, and shifting her seat-cheeks desperately. Then she bowed her head, hiding her face, and yielded her anus to the slim probe.

"Opinions vary," said Dr. Jacobus, "as to whether

vaseline or liquid soap will best prepare a young
woman like Lesley for love. For her lover, the convenience of merely vaselining her is clear. In the present case, where we are dealing with an adulterous
young wife, there is an element of punishment. The
length of the glass squirt and the jet it expels will
stimulate needs and sensations deep in Lesley's backside. Also the light perfume will cause a slight erotic
irritation."

The full length of the squirt was now sheathed in
Lesley's bum, only the black rubber bulb nestling between her hind-cheeks.

"Lie quite still, Lesley," said Dr. Jacobus calmly.
"You must learn to accept these measures of harem
hygiene."

Those who had suffered the arrogance of the
young wife would have relished the face which Dr.
Jacobus obliged her to turn to us. The arrogance had
gone from the blue eyes. Where was the sulky, self-
possession of her clear, fair-skinned features and
firm mouth? He squeezed the black bulb lightly and
her body tensed at the first muffled squirt. There
was a sudden wild-eyed and open-mouthed alarm in
her face. Our haughty young woman seemed to scan
the rows of chairs imploringly for someone who
might intercede on her behalf. She saw only twenty
eager faces. Dr. Jacobus tightened his arm 'round
her waist. He pressed the bulb hard and repeatedly.
With a forlorn cry, Lesley jammed her legs harder
together and tensed her pale bum-cheeks on his busy
fingers. When he had done, he withdrew the glass
probe. Lesley's anus went desperately tight and small
as the glass tip came clear.

"First, gentlemen, let us consider the amorous use
of Lesley's behind. By her promiscuous conduct, she
has lost all right to object to its use in this manner.

Having surrendered herself to her urges, it is only
right that she must surrender to those of others."

There was a ready murmur of assent to the justice
of these remarks, for who could dispute so moral an
argument? Dr. Jacobus resumed. "We are fortunate
in having as our demonstrator one whom I will call
the Schoolmaster. He has long been an admirer of
Lesley's backside as she bent to some task in a pair
of tight riding jeans. Then, alas, she was not a slave
girl and his lust had to be curbed. Let us concede,
however, that he is not a favourite with her. He
lately administered severe chastisement with his cane
to the bare buttocks of a favourite of hers, her
daughter-nymph, while our boyishly cropped Venus
was obliged to listen in the next room!"

This at once made the situation more provoking!
The Schoolmaster appeared in a mask and a waist-
length leather jerkin. His phallus, understandably
stiff with expectation, stood out and nodded as he
walked. He adjusted a mirror so that he would be
able to see Lesley's face while he ravished her arse.
Sitting on the side of the table, he circled her waist
with one arm and looked down on the full, pale
swelling of Lesley's wifely young seat-cheeks. "Your
face to the mirror, Lesley," he murmured. "Watch
yourself being prepared. Try to imagine how much a
man enjoys doing it!"

He took a large blob of vaseline from a jar and
slowly spread it on her tight inward rear dimple. In
her agitation, Lesley twisted her head, looking back
at him beseechingly. Her blue eyes interceded forlornly. The sulky mouth whispered peevishly those
reasons which made her behind so vulnerable to ravishing. He smiled at her with amusement.

"That's your problem, Lesley! My prick is so stiff
that I could not desist merely because you may be

inconvenienced for a day or two! Such shrewishness, Lesley! Your right to choose who beds you? Your body belongs to you? Surely you forget where you are! Such mischievous nonsense is never tolerated from a harem slave-wife!"

His finger diddled the urchin-cropped Venus between her buttocks as she lay on her belly over the rubber cushions. He fondled the smooth, erotic maturity of Lesley's bottom-moons, which were swelled out and broadened by the cushions under her loins.

"Be sensible, Lesley!" he murmured, "it won't be the first time you've been sodomised, will it? You still pretend your husband never dared it in a fit of honeymoon passion? None of your lovers during marriage? Ah, but do not deny that the two Arab traders performed the act on you during your night in their captivity. True, we heard you refuse their suggestion indignantly. But Karim waited long enough to hear you getting it anyway, Lesley! Such cries at first—and then soft sighs. A furtive and guilty thrill as they probed your rear depths, Lesley? A promiscuous young woman soon learns to enjoy it!"

"They *forced* me!" Her resentment had a spoilt child's petulance.

"Your consent is irrelevant here, Lesley. Your master's right over your backside and the rest of you is absolute. Did those two rogues get you into bad habits? I follow their example without compunction!"

"But I can't! I daren't! . . . I won't!"

He stooped, kissing each of Lesley's proud, pale bottom-cheeks.

"The days are past, Lesley, for walking out on marriage and duty to gratify your urges with a lover. The little metal prod heats in the brazier coals. Every poor frustrated harem eunuch longs for the order to draw it out and tantalise your bare bottom with it where my lips now browse! Ah! Your buttocks tighten with alarm at that!"

He paused, then resumed, smiling at her with wicked promise.

"Your rear valley and its tight little crater, Lesley! My lips salute you there . . . and there. Ah, you have underestimated its seductive appeal! At high school and college, did you never imagine a man for whom this would be your great centre of interest?"

"No!" A peevish wail, petulant yet imploring.

"Ah!" Touching Lesley's anus with his finger, he seemed to quess the truth. "Why so tense and tight, Lesley? Too proud to confess the cause? I believe that my shapely young hen is shy of the cock because she wants to lay? Let us see!"

While Lesley's mouth turned down in a woebegone manner, he took a slim, twelve-inch glass rod and slid it gently but deeply into her backside. The young wife gave a little cry as it reached its full depth. The Schoolmaster withdrew it carefully.

"Ah, yes. Not truly desperate, but beginning to be so. Take the rod carefully by this end, footman, and show it to the spectators."

"Oh, please . . . no!" It was Lesley's hopeless protest at seeing the state of her behind thus displayed to the amusement of the onlookers.

"Turn your fringe, Lesley! I must kiss those arrogant blue eyes! Lesley, my love, I taste your first tears upon my tongue! Now, my sweet, the pin-head of the marker is glowing. I shall enjoy caressing you with it between your buttocks, Lesley, unless you can divert me by your submission."

I am sure he would never have done so, Charlie—

would he? But the effect of his words was enough.

"That's better, Lesley! Arch your seat out like that! A little farther! I believe you want it after all! Now, let me kneel astride your thighs—my knob to your anus, Lesley! Ahhhhh!"

He pressed the tight rear dimple inwards until the young wife yielded her arse to him with a short, hollow cry. The Schoolmaster's penis shaft slid deeply inbetween the proud, white cheeks of Lesley's bottom. He drew back a little and plunged again in a vigorous in-and-out. His loins slapped rhythmically upon Lesley's buttocks, his penis driving with all its power into the arse of this promiscuous young wife, punishing her adultery.

"So tense, Lesley? What? Whisper it to me! Ah, the added bulk of the tool compounds your urgency, does it? Put such things from your mind. Tighten your rear muscle rhythmically on my shaft. Exquisite!"

He rode her triumphantly for about ten minutes, at which point Lesley begged him to end the ravishing quickly.

"You abandoned marriage for your own pleasures, Lesley," said he, "now you must abandon yourself to mine. Lie still a moment! My lust shall not boil over for half an hour yet!"

Soon he began again, and later paused. Another beginning, a pause, and so on. Presently, while they lay still and his loins covered Lesley's backside, an involuntary jet of his passion escaped deep in her rear. She made a faint sound of distaste in her throat. He kissed her bare back and was severely logical.

"So prudish, Lesley? The thick warm discharge disgusts you? Such hypocrisy! Why, it is the very substance you begged from your lovers in the warm adulterous passion of your loins! Not quite so snooty about it then, were you, Lesley?"

"I was in love!" Such a sulky schoolgirl wail again.

It was curious, perhaps, that the balm which consummated her illicit passion should so revolt Lesley when squirted into her behind by a man whom she detested. Yet he kissed the crown of her head and his movements began once more.

"You went whoring, Lesley," he murmured, "you deserted the penis of your husband, who had sole legal right to you. Now you shall be punished by mine. Justice requires it!"

"I was in love!" she wailed peevishly, just as before, and as if this excused her.

"You shall be loved here, Lesley," he promised. "The valets will always be waiting in the tiled closet when you needs must go and take your knickers down in there. Karim and Saleh are both lovers of the female backside. Be prepared to bend to their whims before you are permitted to attend to your own."

So the moral agent of retribution rode to his triumph. "Lie still now, Lesley, but arch your bottom out a little farther. I feel the flood breaking the barrier! Lesley, darling! I believe my passion for you is hotter than husband or lover ever felt! Do you feel the squirting in your rear, Lesley? The pulse in your throat beats faster! Ah, you're getting to like it, Lesley, aren't you?"

He lay upon her, not yet drawing his tool from her bum, whispering gently in her ear. To judge from her dismay, he may have been assuring her of his obsessive love for her in this way. Or did her wide eyes testify to how he frightened her with the bogey tales of the harem?—the ultimate demand which lay in

wait for her; the underground room, musicians playing outside to prevent the escape of a chance sound.
The pale moons of Lesley's bottom were presented
for this last rite as if on a pagan sacrificial altar, for
even in extremities his obsession would choose this
way. Whatever the subject, his last words were audible.

"You shiver, Lesley? Did you never wonder if
such things must not happen behind harem walls?"

When the young wife gave a little cry of alarm, it
was because she felt how his own words had hardened him again in her behind. In vain, the boyishly
cropped Venus tried to expel the flaccid serpent. But
Lesley's arse movements, squeezing upon it, had
only stiffened it once more.

"Ready for it again, Lesley? You liked an encore
from your lovers!"

The movements of sodomy resumed. Lesley shook
her parted fringe back to twist her head 'round and
plead that she could scarcely contain the volume of
his first tribute in addition to her own load and the
heavy penis muzzle. There was a faint show of resistance, a smack or two on her legs, his smile meeting
her forlornness as she yielded with a soft cry.

"For your own sake, Lesley, you must be broken
in to this pleasure thoroughly in a few weeks, so that
you may overcome timidity and enjoy it. My valets
shall accompany your morning visit to the tiled
closet. This exercise shall be part of your routine in
there."

She gave a plaintive and yearning little cry at last,
as a morbid and hectic thrill was stirred by the penis
in her bowels. Several of the audience chuckled and
vowed the young bitch was getting a taste for it.
Meanwhile, a soldier had Shawn bending over with
knickers' round her ankles. He kissed the full lips

and the tight-lidded dark eyes of this eighteen-year-old. He kissed his way up the length of her long, elegant, coffee-skinned legs. He kissed the West Indian beauty between her thighs, then on her tautly rounded bum-cheeks. He pressed apart the tawny-gold cheeks of Shawn's bottom and presented his knob to her anus. The way was too narrow without the aid of some unguent. He applied this, pressed her waist down, and spanked hard on Shawn's buttocks. After that, she received him with a wild willingness, randily supplying the movements for her own ravishing.

Peeping through the curtains beside me, I also glimpsed my silver-haired neighbour and his young concubine. Patrizia was bending forward over the rail in front of the seat. He made her keep her face turned so that he might enjoy the appeal of her wide, brown eyes, broad, warm-skinned cheekbones, and dark page-style hair. This appealing Italian tomboy no longer boasted the tight pants whose seat she had filled so broadly and roundly. Now one could admire the bare olive-skinned voluptuousness, the slight heaviness in the cheeks of Patrizia Luisi's bottom. Her eyes were fixed upon her elderly lover's swelling knob. "No is possible!" she gasped, in her charming broken English.

His answer was to stroke scented lubrication between her buttocks. He took his lance in both hands, aimed it, and thrust home. I guessed that her little friend Regina was undergoing a similar ordeal in the next seat. Beyond that, perhaps, was blond Francesca, with her elegant coiffure. Francesca's costume of short, belted tunic in red silk and tight, plum-coloured riding trousers of shiny leather would seal her fate. So, while Patrizia was buggered next to me, sharp-featured little Regina matched her ordeal. Beyond her, blond and sophisticated Francesca bent over, her wifely young anus stretched round her admirer's weapon. Thus, my dear Charlie, I take my leave of you as our learned Dr. Jacobus pauses before the final part of his stupendous experimental lecture.

A bientôt,

Your loving Lizzie

Ramallah, 5 August 1904

My dearest Charlie,

I NOW FIND leisure to write—even
as the events still unfold—to tell you of the conclusion of the lecture by our learned moral philosopher,
Dr. Jacobus. Though past midnight, the courtyard
was brightly lit. The attention of the assembled
scholars never once wandered from the theme.

Lesley remained secured on her belly over the
leather bolster. Her behind was still the centre of attention. Though discipline now replaced passion, the
pale, yellow-grey gobs of vaseline were still visible,
like honey in the comb, between the cheeks of Lesley's bottom. A broad smear of the unguent crossed
one of her seat-cheeks, marking the track of the
Schoolmaster's penis as he withdrew it from her.

"Gentlemen," said Dr. Jacobus solemnly, "we
now come to a scene which must be set in sombre
colours, a theme cast in a minor key. I speak of
chastisement. You need, however, have no misgivings. You will see Lesley punished for adultery in a
manner which law and morality have upheld since
the dawn of civilisation. The whipping of an adulter-

178

ous young wife is an act in which almost all men of sense and honour would concur. Her husband, even the lovers she deserted her marriage for, would want to see the penalty inflicted. In the Arab world our punishment of the whip is lenient by comparison with the vindictive discipline of branding needle or impaling cucumber for Lesley's backside. By the law of many pashas, such retributions are followed by the inexorable tightening of the leather 'Collar of Justice' about the throat. Here we deal more lightly with her."

You may imagine the fright which filled Lesley's arrogant blue eyes under her little-boy fringe at this. Yet she would not suffer more than the ultimate discipline of the prison or school.

Lesley will use every subterfuge to escape justice," continued Dr. Jacobus. "Exaggerated screams to win pity are most common. Unnecessary degrees of twisting and writhing are also intended to mislead. Urgent entreaties will be made to perform certain acts whose needs can no longer be denied. Yet we may defeat such ruses!"

What could he mean? I had no idea.

"We judge by the state of Lesley's bottom," said he. "Therefore we curb her writhing a little. An extra pinion strap above the knees, another at the waist. A gag of damp wadded cotton, held by a thin strap between the teeth and secured at the nape, is doubly advantageous. It reduces the temptation to unnecessary shrillness and protects her teeth against chipping as she clenches in pain."

There was a moment of resistance—pressed lips, mewing, and head-twisting—like a little girl refusing the medicine spoon. But soon the wadded cotton and strap were in place.

"Lastly," said the learned Dr. Jacobus, "in her

frantic endeavour to end the thrashing, she will lose all the self-possessed arrogance of an educated and emancipated young woman. She will perform as shamelessly as a desperate little girl of twelve or thirteen. Of course, the little fountain between her legs has played to exhaustion. Yet Lesley has also implored for some hours a few moments of urgent privacy for another reason. You will, I am sure approve the refusal of such requests, for the ordeal of her punishment is to be increased rather than lightened."

There was a murmur of approval. Dr. Jacobus smiled.

"Indeed, gentlemen, in so distinguished an audience as this, there may be scholars who wish to see the performance of such curious acts. It is prudent, then, to have Lesley in a state where she can display any function of her rear anatomy commanded by you."

He then responded to a ripple of amusement.

"Despite this young woman's appearance of arrogance, she may secretly hope that such commands are given. You may be sure that Lesley would respond to such an order with a show of repugnance and defiance. Her self-respect requires that. Several strokes of the cane would be needed. However greatly she may wish to do it anyway, Lesley will escape the ultimate self-humiliation, if she appears to yield only under the compulsion of the whip."

Like a conjurer, Dr. Jacobus stood before us with a china egg between finger and thumb. It was not quite large enough to tightly fit the necessary place, but it would not be easily dislodged. Lesley twisted her head 'round urgently to watch him, the light catching the fair, straight cut of her crop from its high crown to the severe cutting of it level with her jaw. Dr. Jacobus slid a hand under her, supporting her bare belly. He pressed the oval china egg between her buttocks, the narrower end foremost. There was a tensing of seat-cheeks, and a keening through wadded cotton, while the scholar's mouth set firm and the veins in his forehead stood out more prominently. Lesley's tight inward dimple yielded and closed again over the china oval as it passed up into her behind.

"Observe, gentlemen!" Dr. Jacobus stood back with a flourish. "See how hard and rapid the pulse beat in her throat is. Can it be sexual arousal at the thought of being chastised—or is it no more than a young woman's desperate fright? It matters not at all. Either emotion will generate a pitch of excitement. Lesley feels butterflies in her tummy, as the saying goes, and the flutter of panic in her bowels. The cheeks of her arse are no doubt crawling with such apprehension that they almost itch with it!"

Lesley gave a shake of her little-boy fringe in order to look back at him over her shoulder. It seemed as if the once-disdainful blue eyes were trying to ask a question she could not utter. Her clear, pale features were a study in the most fearful anticipation.

"Ah!" Dr. Jacobus smiled knowingly at her. "Lesley is tormented by a last doubt! Will there be any restriction on the instrument of punishment? Any limit to the number of strokes? I think she can already guess that the answer is in the negative!"

How Lesley tugged at her straps—and all in vain! How she turned her blue eyes and fringe urgently to the audience! Whatever disapproval one may feel for Dr. Jacobus, he had a good deal of reason on his side. Lesley is a mature young woman. Her hips and seat have that slight firming-out which enables her to undergo chastisements that would be unthinkable for a schoolgirl. She has endured regular penis exercise in the marriage bed, the labour of child-bearing, the demands of her lovers. Having willingly incurred such extremes of pleasure and pain, she was scarcely able to object to a whipped bottom as punishment for her infidelities. Indeed, by cutting her fair hair in a rather boyish manner, she was surely asking to be given the sort of thrashing well known in some boys' prisons.

"Presently you will be caned, Lesley," said Dr. Jacobus quietly, "but first I shall mark my personal disapproval of your marital treason by twelve strokes with a snakeskin pony-lash."

Lesley was truly frantic at this. She twisted her head and scanned about her, with blue eyes wide and desperate. In vain, she jerked at the restraining straps. The gag reduced her protests to the same shrill keening, but her pale seat-cheeks were tensing urgently.

Dr. Jacobus took the whip, which consisted of a handle and slim, woven lash about eighteen inches long. He ran his hand briefly over the full moons of Lesley's bottom, smiling at the pale vaseline blobs between them and the peeping vaginal pouch between the rear of her thighs.

"You had your fun with your lovers, Lesley," he said gently. "Was it nice? Was it? Did you wriggle on the adulterer's penis until you almost swooned with the joy of it? Now you shall pay a cruel price for it, you young whore!"

His right arm went back and his lips tightened. The cheeks of Lesley's bottom shifted and squirmed uncontrollably. With an ear-stunning crack, the slim, black lash snaked down, curling and clinging to the bare cheeks of Lesley's backside. A split second's pause was followed by wild mewing and buttocks contorting urgently to contain the naked smart of the leather whip. A scarlet stripe appeared, an S-shaped curve across Lesely's bum-cheeks, dotted by two ruby droplets. Lesley had the firm, young seat-swell of a Spartan soldier-girl. Perhaps it was this which caused such breathless excitement among the audience as she was whipped. Or perhaps it was merely the satisfaction of seeing the boyishly cropped wife punished for her promiscuity and for being an arrogant young bitch. Who can say?

Dr. Jacobus made the whip ring out repeatedly with a savage accuracy across Lesley's bottom-cheeks. Soon her pale buttocks were embroidered by plum-red loops and curlicues. Two! Three! Four! The strokes sang out like pistol shots, each stinging Lesley's arse with a scorpion viciousness. Even the fiery kiss of the leather whip was but a prelude to the swelling torment as the impact of the stroke searched her lingeringly for several seconds afterwards. Vainly she tried to take the strokes on her flanks to spare her bottom. But her hips were too well pinned down for that. She tried to turn each buttock uppermost in turn, but neither of them could elude the lash. She tightened them desperately, until her arse-crack was a thin, compressed line.

Dr. Jacobus put a stop to this by an upward stroke of the woven lash, catching the fatter undercurve of Lesley's seat-cheeks just above her thighs. Frantic to writhe away the anguish, the promiscuous young wife thrust her rump out in a complete display of her rear anatomy. It was at this point that the eyes of Dr. Jacobus gleamed. He aimed the lash with vindictive precision between the cheeks of Lesley's bottom. No refuge was left to her as the whip cracked out again. Eight! Nine! Ten! All the self-possessed sophistication taught her at school and college was stripped from Lesley now. Twice the whip's command was printed between the cheeks of her arse. Neither this, nor the flooding tears in the blue eyes, moved the onlookers to intercede.

One must concede, of course, that Lesley was being punished for the great harm done to others by her conduct. To desert marital duty for illicit pleasures is a crime which law and custom has always punished in this manner. Almost every man—and perhaps most women—would have been pitiless with Lesley now. Under the long, fair parting of her little-boy fringe, Lesley's eyes—once so aloof and dismissive—implored her master vainly.

Smack! Whip-smack! Crack-smack! As the lash caught the inward curve of Lesley's bottom-moons again, every muscle in her thighs went taut and her toes curled with the intensity of the discipline. Once or twice Dr. Jacobus moved to block our view a little, and he paused. An Arab boy ran on and held something to the young wife's nose. The scent of ammonia suggested smelling salts. Who can say? During this process, Lesley's face was level with the boy's loins. Like us, she must have seen the scrap of his loincloth bulging with the stiffness inside. No doubt there was many a wicked smile and knowing whisper from the frisky boy, assuring her of his enthusiasm for seeing her punished.

Indeed, as I glanced up at the windows overlooking the scene, I could make out the faces of the Arab boys pressing eagerly at each one. Here and there a lad stood alone, the movement of his upper arm suggesting that he was busily polishing some object in his hand.

"The justice of chastisement is absolute," said Dr. Jacobus, as he finished. "Lesley has made others suffer in order that she might enjoy her lecheries. What she endures now is a modest retribution."

Lesley twisted her head wild-eyed in dismay, for now the Schoolmaster appeared, cane in hand. Already Lesley's bottom-cheeks blushed deeply, the whip prints raised in slight contours across her backside and the rear of her upper thighs. The boyishly cropped Venus-wife sprawled in her straps like an overgrown schoolgirl or page boy over the cushions of the teacher's sofa.

The Schoolmaster removed the gag, allowing her to lie flatter as well. "I shall not need such expedients," he said. "Besides which, when I cane a bottom, I like to see it writhe! How many canings your parents and teachers neglected, Lesley! How many punishment lessons to make up for before we have trained you to loyalty and submission!"

Lesley emitted a shrill protest, but the Schoolmaster dismissed it. "Come now, Lesley! You have tasted the pony-whip! What greater objection can there be to a reformatory cane? Remember, I have already severely bamboo'd the bare buttocks of your thirteen-year-old filly. Surely that entitles me to thrash the backside of the young mare with my cane, as well?"

There was a good deal of general amusement at this. When the murmurs of laughter died away, the supple bamboo rang out across Lesley's bottom, the weals rising straight across the curving prints of the lash. You may imagine the frenzy of Lesley's screams, deeply gratifying to the moralists who watched her thrashed for adultery. He caned her across the backs of her thighs half a dozen times and then returned to the cheeks of her statuesque young seat.

The Schoolmaster was worthy of the great tradition of pedagogues. Each lash of the cane was given with stern vindictiveness. I doubt if the thirteen-year-

old nymph wept more violently under the bamboo
than the boyishly cropped young Venus of twenty-
eight was doing now. Lesley's backside writhed over
the leather bolster in a manner which was positively
lewd. You might have thought, from its sinuous
squirmings, that her behind was trying to seduce the
chastiser into other pleasures.

In the warm night, the young wife's proud bare
belly slithered on the leather bolster as she squirmed.
There was a faint dry squeak of the restraining straps
as she pulled vainly at her bonds. Under the caning,
the firm, mature cheeks of Lesley's bottom met and
parted in their writhing with a slippery kissing sound
caused by the thickly smeared vaseline between
them.

How would it end? How *could* it end? The
Schoolmaster's disciplinary zeal seemed unabated,
and it was impossible to imagine what would satisfy
his punitive skill. His resolve stood out stiffly as ever
for all to see. Yet now Lesley twisted her head
round. She seemed to be trying to look down the
length of her spine at her own bottom. In truth, she
was directing the Schoolmaster's gaze to that place!
The reply was an expertly aimed lash of bamboo,
drawing blood in pinpricks across several of her earlier weals. Such frenzy was provoked by it! The
atrocious smart of the bamboo caused the rounded
end of the china egg to peep out between Lesley's
bottom-cheeks! Was she about to use the only subterfuge remaining by which she could halt her punishment, if only for a moment?

The Schoolmaster, admirable moralist that he is,
was not to be deflected from his duty by the reap-
pearance of the china egg, which Dr. Jacobus had
inserted in the young wife's behind. Again and again
and supple bamboo lashed across Lesley's buttocks.

The egg grew rounder and larger as it emerged, until it rolled free from Lesley's anus, down her bare legs, and across the demonstration table. An ear-splitting smack of the cane across her statuesque backside brought a frantic pleading to her face again. As the Schoolmaster caned her again and again it seemed that this promiscuous twenty-eight-year-old wife disgraced herself deliberately. The blemish swelled out between her buttocks and hung in a lewd curve down the left cheek of Lesley's bottom!

What of the Schoolmaster when he saw this outrage to discipline? His lips parted in a paroxysm of moral outrage—or was it a grin of delight?—and he gave two more strokes of the cane across Lesley's backside with all his skill. A second swelling blemish dislodged the first. Had one not known how strict a moralist the Schoolmaster was, it might seem that, having seen Lesley's thirteen-year-old filly lift her tail under chastisement, he was determined to drive the young mare to the same extreme.

For all her educated arrogance and emancipated self-possession, Lesley perhaps guessed at the strange vices which bedevil mankind. Her college education, several years of marriage, and a few lovers, had surely taught her some bawdy truths. Did she hope to excite the Schoolmaster to completion by performing the most lewd and utter self-abasement of which her bottom she was capable?

To be sure, it had an effect upon him. The cane dropped from his hand, for he was now obliged to clutch his own stiffness. Lesley turned her brimming eyes and woebegone mouth—a vision in itself enough to cause his orgasm. She was in time to see the Schoolmaster's weapon explode in mid-air, uncontrollably, with the pure exhilaration of his triumph. Thick lusty jets spat forward and liberally bespangled Lesley's backside with arcs of spawn. Who knows? Perhaps the slippery balm soothed her at last.

The Schoolmaster staggered with the exertion of his display. Murmurs of concern for him rose among the spectators, as two soldiers ran forward and supported the valiant pedagogue from the dais. In a spontaneous tribute, the assembled scholars broke into applause. Happily, the Schoolmaster was able to return in a moment. Weeping contritely for her misconduct, Lesley implored him not to cane her again. He knelt to pick up the bamboo. As he did so, Lesley twisted her urchin-crop 'round violently and with tongue fully extended just managed to lick at the Schoolmaster's knob. Her arrogance was conquered now, for we heard her plead like a little girl.

"Please! Please, let me! Oh, please!"

He permitted it, teasing her over her reluctance to perform the same lip service to her husband. At the same time, he left her in no doubt that she was earning a temporary respite at the cost of humiliation presently. As the curtain fell upon the dais, his voice was audible behind it.

"Your tongue under the foreskin as you suck, Lesley! What delights await you when the shaft grows hard again. So randy even in your present state, Lesley? A moment more and I shall make you do something which will shock you profoundly. Can you guess it, Lesley? Yes! I believe you can! The promise of chastisement alone shall ensure your obedience this time."

Dr. Jacobus in turn was the object of prolonged applause. He was recalled repeatedly, smiling and bowing his thanks to the guests. Our generous host, the Pasha of Ramallah, has put his own private bedroom at my disposal. Its secret windows look into adjoining suites, including that of Dr. Jacobus. Now I make my way thither to see what I shall see. Be sure, dearest Charlie, you shall have a full report of the proceedings from your own adoring

Lizzie

Ramallah, 6 August 1904

Charlie! Oh, dearest Charlie!

*T*HIS SHALL be the last, the very last, letter you shall receive from your devoted Lizzie! You will not think me cruel when you know why. Those pages I wrote in such haste last night to describe the experimental lecture lie upon my table. You shall read them one day if you wish, though I scarcely think you will need to! This, which I write now, shall come to you first!

Let me explain, Charlie. I looked through the glass from my own boudoir into that allotted to Dr. Jacobus. The learned doctor was not there—or rather he was just going out of the door with Regina, the sharp-faced little Italian minx with her tumble of dark curls. The other two girls, Patrizia and Francesca, remained. They were accompanied by four of the Pasha's guards, who looked upon them with greedy eyes. Both girls were dressed again. Eighteen-year-old Patrizia, with her stocky prettiness, appealed to the men, with her wide-brown eyes, dark, page-style hair, the broad and high cheekbones of her warm-skinned face. Her softly luscious Italian breasts weighed out the blue silk of her blouse. The tight, denim trouser seat was once again broadly filled by the voluptuous heaviness of the olive-skinned cheeks of Patrizia's bottom. What a sophisticated contrast was Francesca, the young wife of twenty-five! Her blond hair was swept back from her rather sharp profile and blue eyes, and pinned in an elegant coiffure at the back of her head. Her costume, too, was more elegant than the younger girl's. A pink, belted tunic came down to the top of her hips. Below that she was dressed as if for a travestite role in tight and shiny plum-coloured trousers with a sheen like polished leather.

Patrizia is the wide-eyed pleasing tomboy, Francesca the sexually experienced seductress. One of the guards, an Arab lad of fourteen or so, advises her of some blesmish on the tight, leather trouser seat. The young blond woman lifts the back of her tunic, giving him a sight of her elegant, oval bottom-cheeks in the tight, deep-red leather. Looking down over her shoulder, she begins slowly and suggestively rubbing off the blemish from her leather trouser seat with her fingertips. The mere sight of this causes his young weapon to go off, leaving the cheeks of Francesca's trouser seat in a more perilous state than before!

Two men entered at this point, both in carnival masks to conceal their identity from the girls. I had no doubt that the old one was Patrizia's companion during the experimental lecture.

A bench with a padded leather top was at the centre of the floor, and the two Italian girls were facing it on either side. They were required to kneel over it on all fours from opposite sides. Yet they are made to press as close together as possible.

The older man is thus presented with the voluptuous, broadened seat of Patrizia, and the face and ele-

gant coiffure of Francesca. His younger companion,
as he kneels, admires Patrizia's tomboy face and
Francesca's bottom-cheeks and hips tightly clad in
plum-red leather. Each man takes down the pants of
the girl whose rear faces him, so that both are bare
from their waists to their knees. He is thus offered
the mouth of one and the nether body entrances of
the other. The side of each girl's face touches the
bare flank of the other's hip.

Francesca's fair-skinned thighs tense with pleasure
as the young man's tool parts her legs and enters her
warm vagina from the rear. The old man requires
her to suck at the same time, leaving Patrizia entirely
idle. Presently the old roué withdraws from her
mouth and presents his stiffened tool between the
voluptuous, olive-skinned cheeks of Patrizia's bottom. There is some alarm in the wide eyes of her
face, but, though she catches her breath at the outrage, the older man's knob widens Patrizia's arsehole
and his piston is soon engulfed in her behind. The
younger man rides Francesca's cunt for several minutes, then he withdraws and presents himself to Patrizia. There is a moment of shying away before Patrizia sucks at last, leaving Francesca idle as the two
men busy themselves with the eighteen-year-old tomboy.

The older man draws from Patrizia's rear and, in
turn, it is Francesca who—for all her sophistication
and promiscuity—shies away. The older man kneels
patiently, presenting himself, awaiting her compliance. A guard, cane in hand, comes forward. The
bamboo marks the pale, oval cheeks of Francesca's
bottom. The blond coiffure twists, and her hips
squirm. It is suggested that her modesty is merely a
pretence. Her last vestiges of propriety require it to
seem as if she acted under compulsion. The caning

continues until, after a dozen strokes, Francesca opens her mouth widely and wildly for her master, sucking as if her life depended upon it.

Now the young man deserts Patrizia's lips and, taking advantage of Francesca's pale, bamboo'd seat, stretches her rear dimple 'round his shaft. After ten minutes of arse exercise for Francesca, he draws away. Now you may imagine how Patrizia's brown eyes widen, how her protests come through pressed lips.

The guard with the bamboo can scarcely believe his good fortune. His cane smacks down across the width of Patrizia's bottom, so voluptuous. Almost twenty strokes before the cries and tears lead to a tremulous parting of the lips and the weight of the young man's penis, pressing on Patrizia's tongue.

You will imagine, Charlie, that even now I gloss over some of the grosser details. You know, I am sure, that the two girls were not entirely unwilling, and that some of their defiance was assumed in order to heighten the drama by the use of the bamboo. My reason for thinking this was seen in the last act. The two men lay down on their backs upon a pair of padded benches. The two girls lay face down, Francesca on the younger man and Patrizia on the elder. Both their Italian cunts were impaled on the stout tools, and the girls themselves were to provide all the motion. Over each bench stood a guard with a cane, who thrashed the backside of the girl presented to him by these postures.

Francesca's pale, oval buttocks were soundly caned and you might think that Patrizia's darker, heavy-cheeked arse was bamboo'd with exceptional cruelty. Both girls cried with the anguish of the bamboo, and yet with pleasure at the same time. Patrizia came twice and Francesca four times, before the guards at length laid down their switches, as the two masters pumped molted passion into their slave girls' vaginas.

The two libertines resigned the Italian beauties to the guards and turned away. It was then that I heard the younger man speak to the older through his carnival mask. "Well, Uncle Brandon, may the deuce take me if that isn't the best night's work that a fellow ever did. I can't say that even Lizzie should ever know quite all of it from me! Have you ploughed enough now, old fellow? No? Shall we take Nabyla and Jenny Khan to the next room and roger 'em the same way? Or shall we bed them separately?"

I swooned, Charlie, as perhaps they have told you. Carried to bed, I now write this last letter. But *why* did you not say that you were to be at the demonstration lecture. Did they not tell you? This moment two letters arrive for me in your dear hand, telling of the drama of Noreen and your life as a fugitive. Are you now still in bed with Nabyla, my sweet? Stay there! For I am coming, Charlie, and shall bring this last letter in my own person.

Lizzie

The Postscript

With this last charming note, the correspondence between our two young friends comes to a conclusion. Yet their frolics were not quite over, as I may testify, because I have been their companion these past few weeks at Ramallah, preparing the letters for publication.

Many mysteries were revealed, not least the truth about that delightful old rogue, Uncle Brandon. The frisky old fellow was alive and well when Charles heard of his death and was summoned to Gray's Inn. In truth, it was the old man's bank balance rather than his health which was on the wane. He had withdrawn abroad to Arabian climes, where he consoled himself with a seraglio of bare beauties. In his desperation, he saw how easily a penny might be turned by supplying his wealthy Arab neighbours with English girls who would cost them dear at auction. In Greystones, he discerned an unending source of supply.

Miss Martinet was most accommodating in the matter, for old Uncle Brandon had given her a fuck or two which still tickled the rim of her cunt a year later. Maggie and Noreen, Jackie and Mandy, Tania and Shawn, were but a few of the young ladies from Greystones who were judged worthy of release on condition of taking up employment with ladies or gentlemen who were just en route for the Middle East.

The enterprise prospered until there was that certain difficulty with Noreen. Thereafter, both Charles and Miss Martinet were obliged to follow rather hastily in the footsteps of Uncle Brandon. By the happiest touch, it was the cadaverous old brief of Gray's Inn, Silas Raven, who was apprehended for impropriety. To his great good fortune, he had been at Eton with the Attorney General and recollected vividly how the Attorney General at thirteen was a devil for sucking the prick of every other boy in the school, including several members of the present cabinet. The prosecution was hushed up for fear of what old Silas might divulge. I thus came safe to the Pasha of Ramallah and was kindly installed in a favoured suite with windows into the other rooms.

Let me confess that, like Lizzie, Charlie, and the Pasha, I am a libertine. Our own pleasures and those of our companions form our rule of life. Yet compared with the moralists who infest this place, we are innocents indeed.

The young English Milord is a builder of empire, his place in the House of Peers awaiting him. He deals severely with warm-skinned beauties like Jennifer Khan or Nabyla Justo, over whom he will one day rule. Do you recall his frolic with Connie, the Chinese maiden, during Pasha Ibrahim's carriage exercise? It will not surprise you to learn that I glimpsed this young aristocrat, through one of my secret windows, exercise his skill upon the delectable

Miss Carol Jolly. At twenty-years-old, she has the trim figure and sharp features of a lynx-eyed temple dancer. That warm, gold tan might be Grecian or Arabian, with sloping brow and nose, a short crop of lightly curled dark hair brushed upward. How slender the gold neck and the neat whorls of ears bare for kissing!

Her straight, slender back and neat breasts rise from a narrow waist. From her knees a pair of slim and outward-branching thighs rise to her trim but agile hips. When she bends or kneels forward, the tautly but lasciviously rounded cheeks of Miss Jolly's bottom are wantonly and deeply separated by her trim thighs' outward slope.

They tell me she first caught Milord's attention when he was a mere pupil who chanced to see her brushing a carpet on all fours—or was it polishing a harness-room floor? He was then only Master Henry, not Milord. Now, as I watched them, he had her at his absolute disposal. He liked to see Miss Jolly's trim figure in close-fitting singlet and even tighter riding jeans.

Sitting in his chair, he made her kneel before him. The golden-skinned line of brow and nose, the meek mouth and chin, the tight-lidded almond eyes, were bowed to his trouser front. Raising her hips from her heels, going on all fours to give better suck, Miss Jolly's tongue ran over the penis knob and then took it in her mouth.

Her cheeks hollowed inward a little as she sucked eagerly upon his erection. The tight-lidded almond eyes and the high arch of her brows added their own appeal to the smooth Levantine gold of her complexion. He made Miss Jolly suck the penis for some while, before leading her to a low, padded stool fastened to the floor. Over this heavy support, he made her kneel on all fours, strapping her down upon it securely by her waist and wrists. From the rear, one admired the tight jeans, as they moulded the lasciviously rounded and delectably parted cheeks of Miss Jolly's bottom. Gently he pulled these pants down and her singlet up, fondling the neat, pale-gold cherry-topped breasts.

He pinioned her ankles and strapped her slim, tawny thighs together just above the knees. Then, bowing down, he adjusted his mouth to the rearward pout of the love-purse at her thighs. He kissed the warm, coppery smoothness of her upper legs and then began to run his tongue pitilessly in her young vaginal slit. A randy young piece like Miss Jolly could not hope to conceal her feelings at this. The beautiful Turkoman mask of her face faltered in expressions of swooning ecstasy. From time to time, his lips browsed on the velveteen yellow-brown of the small of her back, on the coppery satin of her buttocks. Presently he pressed apart the smooth, copper-toned ovals of her bottom-cheeks. For ten minutes more, he moulded long, exploratory kisses to Carol Jolly's anus. Her dark, almond eyes widened and wandered in astonishment. Yet our randy little wriggler arched her waist down and opened her arse-crack more fully for this unusual attention!

The sequel was not in doubt, even before he unscrewed a jar of vaseline and spread a blob of it upon her tight, dark bum-button. Yet he was no barbarian who would put her to the sacrifice at once. Smiling at her knowingly, he first kissed her slanted, odalisque eyes, her high brow, her sharp young nose, her neat ears, and the nape of her neck, laid bare by her upward-brushed curls. But now he was resolute, determined to brook no refusal. Her mouth quivered as the hammerhead of his passion knocked for admission at the tight, inward dimple between her buttocks. She gave a gasp, then a short, hollow cry. Milord's mouth was set tight as he pressed, and the veins of his forehead swelled a little as he forced Miss Jolly's arse, obliging her to strain to accommodate his bulk. Kissing her ear and whispering to her encouragingly in his smiling way, he now threaded deeper. She gave a little fluttering call of dismay at the deepness of his penetration. Then he was embedded to the hilt between the pale Arabian-gold cheeks of Carol Jolly's bottom! One could understand the alarm in her eyes when one saw how hard her arsehole was stretched 'round the base of his stout phallus.

He began to sodomise Miss Jolly gently at first, smiling in his triumph at her timorous backward almond-eyed glances. There was misgiving in the feline elipse of her dark eyes, in conflict with a certain morbid excitement at the sensations he was provoking inside her. Presently, she bowed her crop of dark ringlets and hollowed her waist down to open her behind more fully and take him deeper. Then the lascivious young piece began to copulate with her arse, moving her hips to match her lover's rhythm.

Was it pure randiness? I think it may have been! Yet she perhaps wished also to spur him on to completion before soreness overtook whatever thrills she was now having. So Milord, teeth set in passion's fit, pumped his lust deep and true into Miss Jolly's trimly rounded backside.

You think I have deceived you? You think he is a mere libertine like the rest of us? Not a moralist at all? You are quite mistaken. In a moment you will see Milord Henry worthy of imperial greatness.

Now, in a cooler mood, he sees how such a golden-skimmed temptress deserves retribution for seducing a young proconsul from his duty. He takes a two-foot cord whip, with wooden handle, and goes to release a long-held flow of dinner water. Milord and his kind have strong appetites. Returning, the whipcord well soaked, he teases Miss Carol Jolly by drawing it lightly across her pale-gold buttocks, which tighten with instinctive fear at the wet menacing caress! He calls her a randy little piece, again, and a lascivious little wriggler. Are these not high crimes against imperial morality? Do they not merit a whipping? Observe her, moreover! See how lewdly she kneels over the stool! The taut and saucy roundness of Miss Jolly's bottom-cheeks, well parted by her branching thighs and hollowed waist, is cause alone for the whip.

With a *crack-smack*! the wet whipcord snakes across the cheeks of her bare backside. The tight-lidded almond eyes grow wide, and Miss Carol Jolly screams at the naked anguish of the bottom-flogging. How bitterly she must rue having opened her arse so fully for copulation and now, being tightly strapped, unable to tense its cheeks together! *Whip*! . . . *Whip! Whip-smack!* . . . *Crack-smack!* . . . *Whip-crack-smack*! Her shrill cries are matched by the raised weals and ruby trickles upon her behind. A dozen strokes and the overture is scarcely complete. A dozen more and only the first act of the drama has passed. Then a variation: can he resist a well-aimed crack-shot or two between Miss Jolly's buttocks, the whipcord seeking out her most intimate arse anatomy? It seems he cannot!

There is, however, an entr'acte in the drama—be sure the drama it will resume presently—in order to make the punishment last longer. Our devotee lights his cheroot and takes his leisure. He kneels behind his pretty culprit, who turns her brimming almond

eyes upon him. Milord draws the Havana to cherry
brightness. He shows her this and thereby causes un-
precedented panic in the features of the lynx-eyed
young beauty. For so absolute an imperialist, there is
a suggestive association between the cherry tip of a
glowing cheroot and the bare, coppery cheeks of
Carol Jolly's bottom! To be sure, not all imperialists
regard the matter in this light. To some, the sacrifice
of Havana is unthinkable. Does not Mr. Kipling tell
us that a woman is only a woman but a good cigar is
a smoke? Heedless of such advice, Milord's arm
steadies her 'round the waist. He touches the shim-
mering glow to the pale, Arabian-gold smoothness of
one of Carol Jolly's bottom-cheeks, touching and
stroking lightly. He answers her protests with promises to colour up her seat-cheeks and cause her backside to blush so deeply that it will be a week before
the embarrassment fades.

You are shocked that he should employ such
methods on his young slave girl? You forget that
Milord is a ruler of nations. You truly blame his an-
tic with whipcord and cheroot? Yet when his armies
slaughter ten thousand imperial subjects in battle,
you will praise him for a great victory.

Perhaps there are other moralists who would per-
suade you to leave the ways of the libertine. You
may take your choice here. What of the learned Dr.
Jacobus, that master of moral science? You might
watch his antics through these private windows here.
See, this is one which looks into the tiled toilet suite.

This time it is Noreen, on hands and knees, who
plies the cloth and bucket. No one denies that this
nineteen-year-old strumpet is a suitable object of disciplinary zeal. See her straight, strong back and bold,
young breasts in the clinging singlet. Observe the impudence in her strong, pale features and brown eyes,

in the flick of her dark fringe as the straight hair brushes her collar. Observe the pale-blue jeans cloth, drumskin-tight, over firm, muscled thighs and the sturdy statuesque cheeks of Noreen's bottom!

Dr. Jacobus observes her too. He watches her at her task. Noreen shakes her level fringe clear and stares back at him with contempt. She squirms in the grip of the two valets as they place her on her belly over another fixed stool on the tiled floor, securing her so that Noreen too is conveniently and tightly strapped on all fours over the apparatus.

Now Jacobus is no imperialist tyrant. He believes in the virtues of discipline and purity. Noreen shakes back her dark hair and cranes 'round at him. Jacobus squats, admiring how the tight jeans seat moulds the firm, big cheeks of Noreen's arse. He undoes her belt and lowers the jeans. Now he can tighten extra straps 'round her thighs. His long, learned nose approaches the dividing cleft of the pale, sturdy mounds of Noreen's buttocks.

"Ever had a punishment enema before, Noreen?" the sage inquires. "No? You'll get one every day from now on until your manners improve. Two quarts. Three, if your insolence persists."

He takes a penis-shaped nozzle, soaps it, and threads it deep into Noreen's behind. A tube runs up from it to the stand above, the stand as yet empty. Noreen's impudence falters, for her ordeal has the dread of the unknown.

Dr. Jacobus leaves her for a moment, during which Noreen squirms her head desperately to see the apparatus of punishment. He returns with a large, two-quart glass jar, made for this purpose. Grinning at her, he makes Noreen look into its contents. Leavings of the Arab boys' tosspots and the guards' spitoons, no doubt, with other copious contributions from Tania, Maggie, and Julie. Making Noreen watch, he adds the contents of the liquid soap bottle at the hand basin.

"One quart, Noreen, to begin with. Then the birch for ten minutes. Then the second quart. Then the birch again. The nozzle to remain in place for quite half an hour."

At nineteen years old, Noreen is a quite tall and strongly made girl. Yet the straps are stout enough to render this vain. Jacobus places the jar on the stand, attaching the rubber tube with a clamp upon it. He pauses, having leisure to kneel and fondle his culprit. Under the pretext of adjustment, he buggers Noreen with the nozzle while his other hand tickles her love-pouch.

"Now you shall be punished, Noreen," he says at last, "with a bellyache to drive the insolence from you!"

He releases the clamp and the noxious flood surges down the tube and up Noreen's bottom, into her tripes. She cries out in dismay, and laments her aching guts. Jacobus grins with moral gratification. Seizing the triple-switched prison birch, he thrashes the back of her knees and up the rear of her strong, young thighs. Despite the tube running out from between them, he can birch the pale sturdy cheeks of Noreen's bottom with great vigour. He raises a weal with every swish, continuing until the two mounds of Noreen's arse are birched raw. Then the clamp is removed a second time and Noreen screams even before the effect of the surging flood makes itself felt. Groaning under the labour pains of her double arse-load, she endures a second prison birching.

Noreen, a strapping young wench of nineteen, is strong enough to eject the nozzle by arse contractions before the time is up. With what results! Maddened by the birching, she emits a fountain gush from her rear, soaking her seat, her legs, and the floor around her. As she lies forward on her belly over the stool, thrashed and exhausted, the fruit of Jacobus' zeal peeps rudely out from Noreen's behind! In his triumph, he thrashes dementedly with the birch until the proofs of his victory lie in a lewd curve down Noreen's bottom-cheeks. How the moralist clutches himself at this! The thick and juicy salvos of his passion add a further adornment to the state of Noreen's backside.

Do I deceive you still? You would be a moralist but not of a kind like Dr. Jacobus? Then surely you must join the Schoolmaster, who represents virtue in all its severity. Nor will you object to his subject: the chastisement of a young wife for adultery and willful promiscuity. Be a moralist and yet condone such crimes of hers as these? Impossible. This time, therefore, you shall see a moralist to whom only we poor libertines could object.

Observe the view through the next private window. You see? The culprit is Lesley, an emancipated suburban wife, twenty-eight years old. Nor is the Schoolmaster averse to a public exercise of virtuous vengeance. An entire gathering of moral disciplinarians is assembled to watch as guests of the Pasha.

But first peep through the spy-hole beyond. Before the public chastisement, Lesley is in a room with two of the Schoolmaster's minions, hung like true Arab stallions. This urchin-cropped Venus deserted her husband's penis, as Jacobus once remarked, and must therefore be punished by the tools of others.

Lesley is bare from the waist down, and her cunt is threaded by Saleh's agile prick. He kisses her long, parted fringe of fair hair and her aloof blue eyes, as he does so. He reminds her of the harem penalty for any future infidelity: Nabyla's sharp little knife pruning away the love-lips and clitoris until there is nothing left for her to play with. Simultaneously, Karim fondles the full, pale moons of Lesley's bottom, firmed out by her two babies. The sodomy begins. He makes Lesley milk him with rhythmic contractions of her anus as his tool plunges into her behind. He murmurs in her ear the while, describing the penalty traditionally exacted in this part too for any betrayal of her duty to her master's bed. They must hold her naked and bending while a baby cucumber is oiled then boldly inserted up Lesley's backside until her wickedly distended anus closes over it and it disappears. Her fate is to be caught between the discomfort of it within her and the anguish of its expulsion. Yet expel it she must, held on her belly over the divan, in a long and tormenting parody of birth.

Saleh continued to harry her cunt while Karim sodomises her. When both are done, she is taken at once through the door, beyond which the guests await her. Be sure she is naked from the singlet hem at her waist to her bare feet. A tall stool is bolted to the floor. Over this they bend her forward tightly. Her wrists, waist, and ankles are strapped firmly down, with a final strap pinioning her legs together just above the knees. Soon the voices of the moralists begin.

A pair of well-dressed older women pause as they pass behind the bending young adulteress. Their shrivelled lips purse censoriously at the sight of the love juice still slippery on her firm, white thighs. Their eyes gleam with outrage and delight as they observe the tell-tale yellowed smear of grease between the pale cheeks of Lesley's bottom. Their voices are raised for her to hear and their smiles meet her eyes vindictively.

"The state of her thighs! And see between her buttocks! The wanton young slut has even seduced the loyal guards by offering herself as a young matron of Sodom! These emancipated young wives with their educated ways—they have no shame! Married seven or eight years, you say, Pasha? A child-birth or two? Disgraceful! How one would like to see her truly flogged for such promiscuity!"

Lesley turns the high crown of her short-cut, fair hair, her startled eyes searching those of the two venerable lady moralists. Their smiles are full of wicked promise. The one who speaks lays a richly ringed hand on the firm, young maturity of one of Lesley's bottom-cheeks.

"Permit me, Pasha. My coachman who waits outside has a fine, thin switch of supple whalebone cased in leather. The most recalcitrant of my carriage-ponies is brought to obedience by half a dozen strokes across the rump. In the ordinary course of events, its use on a young wife of twenty-eight would hardly be prudent. Such tales she might tell! Happily, Lesley's complaints will not be heard! Moreover, its use is surely justified on a young woman who abandons home and duty for adulterous passion? See how that mature young bottom of hers is so conveniently presented for prolonged and expert chastisement. With those two seat-cheeks to work upon, one would take Lesley far beyond the frontier of what the world at large calls punishment!"

The Pasha of Ramallah inclines his head in a gracious gesture of assent. Lesley's bare seat and hips squirm vainly in her straps, her buttocks and upper thighs on doubt crawling with a fearful and unendurable anticipation. The blue eyes under the fair, little-boy fringe grow frantic with apprehension. Her sulky mouth is open in a little gasp of alarm. To the satisfaction of the moralists, her arrogant features are now animated by fright. The elderly woman continues to discourse to her host on matters of discipline.

"If I may be so bold, Pasha, a damp wad of cotton, held in place by a strap as a gag, might be judged prudent. My English maid, Nerissa Gray, shall ply the smelling salts."

The Schoolmaster settles down to watch. He summons a nymph of thirteen, with solemn blue eyes and fair tresses, to sit on his naked manhood as he watches. As she slips off her schoolgirl skirt and pants, he remarks that Rachel's bottom already resembles that of a real young lady. To ensure her excitement at the scene before them, his hand moves between her thighs. "Is that nice, my pet?" he murmurs, "is it? Ah, I think it is! Watch them whip her for adultery! Ah, is that nice just there? Move your bottom a little so that the stiffness lies between its cheeks. Is that better? Yes? Watch the punishment, my sweet. Ah, did that hot wet splash startle you? I fear I must deluge you there in a moment! Blame the young adulteress for that! The sight of those firm bottom-moons of hers, striped and squirming under the leather pony-switch! No tears, now. Try to come while you watch, my pet. . . ."

Do you begin to doubt the purity of our Schoolmaster's moral resolve? Still, you cannot deny that of the well-dressed older woman, as a pause occurs in Lesley's whipping.

"Reason suggests, Pasha, that Lesley will be a more submissive slave-wife if she bears indelibly the print of her master's ownership. These two little discs—without which I never travel—are no larger

208

than coins. Yet they have such ingeniously variable
lettering. See, now I make them assume your name
and hers. They will heat to white without melting.
And notice how conveniently Lesley bends just now!
Tradition dictates the inward edges of her buttocks
as the rational place for her slavery to be marked.
Concealed when she stands upright. Visible for inspection when she bends. Her absolute submission
will be easier to her after this. She will even grow
proud to bear the sign of your conquest. Even
though it be secret from others, a backward glance at
her mirror will cause her to stop and admire. You
would consent, sir? It shall be my privilege to supervise the proceeding."

You think such morality—or libertinage—is rare?
I assure you that is not so. Consider Lesley's husband and lovers. To the world they may deplore
loudly and angrily her abduction and sale into slavery. Yet, if given the chance, would not each of them
bribe the guards handsomely for a long farewell keyhole peep at her in her present ordeal? She being lost
to them anyway, would they not gaze in stiffening
admiration at the artful tapestry of the leather switch
across the pale moons of Lesley's bottom? Remember, too, what they may have endured from her self-
possessed arrogance and willful promiscuity. Would
they not, as a result, choose this final keyhole peep
rather than a last tender interview and soft embrace?

What the young wife now undergoes is, by tradition, the revenge of a betrayed husband. Imagine
him, the keyhole spy, watching the bellows blow the
brazier coals. The young wife's long trim thighs,
strapped tightly together, and the pale firm cheeks of
her backside as she bends, are presented to his gaze.
The straight fair hair of her urchin-crop is turned.
How changed are the aloof blue eyes, the fair-

skinned features, the sulky mouth, as she stares in a fascination of horror at the brazier coals and the small, lettered discs! Ten long minutes pass before the elderly guardian of young wives' morals is satisfied with the rose-red brilliance of the discs. During this time, the strapped thighs tense and shift compulsively. The witnesses admire the taut maturity of this emancipated housewife's backside, shaped by love, marriage and child-rearing. Yet its cheeks squirm uncontrollably, as if seated bare on the most tormenting prickle of horsehair. Lesley pleads her case with all the woeful urgency of a twelve-year-old schoolgirl ordered by her teacher to the whipping room.

Be assured that the wronged bridegroom at the keyhole would not intervene if he could. Such is conjugal morality! Indeed, he is obliged to unbutton himself for comfort, caring not who sees. The elderly woman's fur-clad arm goes 'round Lesley's waist to steady the subject. Her maid plies the smelling salts. Every moral gentleman in the room is driven to seek comfort for his excitement. With her other hand, the elderly woman chooses the smooth, yellowed ivory skin on the left-hand slope of Lesley's bottom-crack. She presses down the heated disc and holds it steady during several seconds of wadded frenzy.

Jilted husbands and lovers at their keyholes are true moralists now. Each clutches his stiffness ecstatically. The discs return to the coals for the task is only half completed. Our moral voyeurs are beside themselves with expectation. Mouths open and eyes wide, they await the turning of the other cheek for the rest of Lesley's arse markings, signing the seal of slavery.

To be sure there are libertines present. Yet how innocent they are by contrast. Arab boys, fourteen or fifteen years old, crouch in every shadow and corner of the room. As the whip is fetched, and Lesley twists her urchin-crop frantically, each lad directs her forlorn blue eyes to the stiffness in his hand. Whispering randily, each one urges Lesley to turn her behind a little more in his direction so that he may have a more exciting view of it under the lash. It is the strong sap of youth, not moral humbug, which stirs such excitement in these Arab boys.

You would rather be a libertine than join cause with moralists of this kind? My felicitations on your choice! What awaits you then?

Be sure there will follow an auction of such beauties as you have seen. Linda and Valerie, Vanessa and Elaine, Noreen and Maggie, Nabyla and Connie, Patrizia and Lesley. All shall appear on the dais and go under the hammer. Lord of the world of fancy, you may purchase as you choose. Yours, too, the choice of pleasures which you may enjoy in the harem of your dreams with these chosen beauties. Perhaps you will be more ingenious still. Shall your palace of love contain several pleasure domes, each filled with young odalisques expert in some skill or to be submitted to some caprice of yours?

Will there be one where Linda and Francesca greet you with parted lips and agile tongues? Is there a second, where Linda and Valerie offer you the warm avenue of pleasure between their legs? Can there be a third, in which two sturdy young women, like Maggie and Noreen, bend to offer their behinds for your entry? Must Elaine and Lesley languish in a fourth, bending for discipline? Perhaps you will be content to mingle demands among your girls. Perhaps you will demand a single favourite pleasure from them all.

As the auction begins, which fair damsels shall be

your choice? Before you stand the two most youthful, each in her school blouse and tie with short, pleated skirt. Such a pleasing contrast. Linda, the softly shaped little blonde, with pale face and sly green eyes. Observe her press the short blond mane to her mouth and snigger with the furtiveness only possible in a minx of fourteen. Her classmate, Valerie, is the slim, freckled gamine with a bob of auburn hair and lively blue eyes. She has the pretty giggling manner of her age.

What an academy of love you might set up with such pupils! Yet surely Linda and Valerie, as a pair of pretty third formers, may enjoy tuition together on your bed! Thus your own hands remove their skirts, their warm schoolgirl knickers and blouses. Gently you will fondle the young breasts, your kisses browsing on each pair of lips in turn. When your hand slips between their legs and masturbates each soft furry little creature, you will find different reactions. Linda, the sly sensuous little blonde, will be greedy for this. Valerie, the slim freckled gamine, with her auburn bob and freckles, is more nervous and tense. As you bring ecstasy between Valerie's slim thighs, there may be sobs and tears at sensations beyond her control. But she will learn to subude this.

Linda, your soft sensuous little blonde, will snigger at the sight of your penis, unlike Valerie, who looks so apprehensive. You may judge from this that Linda, at fourteen, is ready to suck the prick, and this you will require. Must Valerie follow the example, hesitantly? The decision is yours. As Linda's blond head bows, sucking your staff of life, will you require her to complete her submission in this manner? Or will you choose some other way? The world is evenly divided in its opinion of the ripeness of two such girl-cherries for plucking. Yet no two are alike.

So perhaps, after Valerie sucks, Linda turns on her back.

How seductive she looks in her school uniform, lying on her side on the bed, the blond mane pressed knowingly to her lips! Again, as you lie behind her, you will undo the short, pleated skirt and lower it. Her plump young seat-cheeks are tightly shaped by the white web-cotton of her schoolgirl knickers. You ease down these pants and admire your fourteen-year-old Venus. The plump, pearly little moons of Linda's bottom are at your disposal to lodge your stiffness between or to press deeper.

Or will you play the pedagogue, displeased with a pair of sniggering and giggling young madams? You are the school tyrant to whom the gamine with auburn bob and blue eyes appears, carrying a note. It requests the birch-rod across the slim, bare cheeks of Valerie Bishop's bottom. Or the pale pearly cheeks of Linda Jennings' bottom. You have them side by side, two raised and bare seats presented over the sofa back. I shall not be surprised to learn that eighteen strokes of the birch sufficed you for Valerie, but, in Linda's case, three dozen with a bamboo was scarcely enough!

Nor will your collection be complete without a demure older houri. Before you on the auction dais appear warm-skinned beauties of eighteen or twenty: Patrizia, Jennifer, Connie, and Nabyla. Connie, with her high-boned Chinese beauty and her long sheen of black hair with silver clips, is a study in submissive loveliness. Connie's knickers are tight, black silk on saffron-smooth skin, as she lies obediently upon the bed. How those loving slanted eyes beseech you as she unbuttons and releases your sex, asking demurely to be allowed to suck it! You cannot refuse. Connie slips down her pants and plays with herself as she does so, moistening the way between her legs for your next pleasure. Then, as she turns, will you birch the delicate saffron cheeks of Connie's Chinese bottom or allow her to part those cheeks with her own hands to offer you yet another form of enjoyment—or will you do both?

Can you resist Miss Jennifer Khan, the Asian beauty? Such high-boned cheeks, smouldering almond eyes, pretty tangle of black hair lying between her shoulders? As you undress her on the bed, Jennifer's knickers are tight-stretched briefs of white cotton-web. How they contrast with the tawny stockiness of her bare thighs! You tongue-flick the Asian beauty's nipples to erection. Your tool threads into her cunt while she responds like a wild-cat. Perhaps you would be prudent to strap her wrists to the bedrail for her passion knows no limits! Then turn her over and fondle the proud, olive-skinned cheeks of Jennifer Khan's bottom! Though her finger bears a betrothal ring, you may be sure she is virgin in almost every respect. You cannot endure to miss a single enjoyment? Then press apart those tawny-skinned seat-mounds and press until the very root of your penis is gripped exquisitely by Jennifer Khan's arse-hole! Does her high and fiery temper boil over in disobedience at this? At nineteen, she should know better. Later on, she is kneeling with head touching the pillowing. Do you choose to employ the snakeskin pony-lash across her bottom to an extent undreamt of in reformatory or school? That is your privilege, if you wish, and your pleasure, if you choose.

Here we touch again on that most profound topic of "Birch in the Boudoir," for there is no other which shows so clearly the difference between a moralist and a libertine. Can you resist purchasing a reformatory tomboy of fourteen like Elaine, as she is led on to the dais? She is defiant and impudent—is not that what you want? The fair hair, combed from its central parting to lie loose upon her shoulders, frames the broad oval of her face. Narrow eyes and thin mouth complete the picture of snub-nosed insolence. Consider her in school blouse and tie, pleated, grey skirt worn scandalously short to bare her robust young thighs.

Among your other attractions, would you not like Elaine upon your bed, her wrists duly strapped to the rail? A moralist would be as eager as you, but would pretend he found no pleasure in it. You ignore her curses as you stoop over and fondle those bare white thighs, sturdy and adolescent, below the hem of her skirt. Quietly you lay a bamboo to soak in mustard oil, where she can see it. You detach and lower the little skirt. Elaine Cox's schoolgirl knickers are the only type possible under so short a skirt: briefs of white, stretched cotton. You ease them down over her robust young hips. Such strong young thighs, the fair hair at the loins, the pouch well fleeced. Yet you may wonder how many a lucky lad of her own age has discovered such things before! As you change sides, lying down behind her, she tosses her fair hair and cranes 'round with all the snub-nosed impudence of her kind. Your face level with her hips, you pull the blouse tail high and fondle the full, pale cheeks of your fourteen-year-old tomboy's bottom. A virginity to be had here? Is it taken while Elaine protests with hollowed mouth and constricted cries? Yet here we have no moralising, only a call to love's arms. "You've a strong young bottom, Elaine. Any pasha would start early with you!"

When the cane is taken from the mustard oil, if

that is your choice, there is no cant about discipline. It will be done only because you enjoy it. Indeed, it will be in the small hours of the morning for you will have been occupied with her in other ways and your tool will scarcely have left her behind before midnight.

Once more, you will cane Elaine Cox's tomboy bottom with a severity unknown to any school. Yet her teachers would all be libertines enough to envy you. Elaine may be a strapping youngster for fourteen years old. Once again, however, the criterion is not her fitness for such discipline but your desire to give it. You may reprieve her after half a dozen strokes, or continue until Elaine's buttocks are a willow pattern of swelling weals. Still you are not satisfied? The cane lashes down across the fattish surfaces of Elaine's bottom-cheeks as if across ripe fruit. But let us have no cant about moral discipline, for the penis standing stiff and bare at your loins will contradict you!

Let me put no limit on your choice as the beauties parade before you. Maggie and Noreen, Tania and Julie, whichever you choose shall be added to your ideal harem. Yet would you show the superiority of the libertine over the moralist? Then take Lesley and show how she may be subdued through passion rather than vindictiveness.

A man who owns such a seraglio will make several of his favourites slave-wives. Lesley is surely eligible. See her on your bed, naked but for the tight, black straps at wrists, waist, ankles, collar, and 'round the middle of each thigh. The penalties for refusal ensure her compliance in acts which are to prove as much her pleasure—it is to be hoped!—as yours. Can you resist including in the celebration the thirteen-year-old nymph with such solemn blue eyes and fair hair? Two such haughtily solemn faces. One pair of thighs still so so slim and resilient, the belly so flat; the other mature thighs, firm but proud, the belly a little rounded. Turn them over. Compare the backside of the boyishly cropped Venus of twenty-eight and her blue-eyed daughter of thirteen. The graceful slimness of the woman-child seat-cheeks and the proud bottom-moons of the mature young wife!

While nimble fingers play between her legs, Lesley will soon learn to enjoy those sessions, when she bows her urchin-crop and sucks the stiff penis presented to her lips. The pumping of your warm passionate gruel, which caused her to retch at first, she will learn to swallow by repeated lessons. You fear, however, that Lesley, having been content with a variety of pricks in her cunt before, will never be happy with yours alone? Have no fear! Yours is the only one, and she will adore it all the more for that!

Sometimes you will stir in the night and find that the young wife lies on her side with her back to you. Move gently down the bed till your eyes are level with her seat and the rear opening of her thighs. Observe the rear of her vaginal purse as it pouts back and you will find it exuding pearly droplets. Lesley is masturbating furtively, despite your own use of her cunt, despite the yellowed grease smears between her bottom-cheeks, where you sodomised this young wife as well. Under the aloof exterior—the clear blue eyes, dismissive snootiness, and boyish fringe—Lesley yearns for love.

You will sodomise Lesley, of course. Perhaps it will be more frequent than the more orthodox pleasure, for it risks no swollen belly. Having carried two infants already, a third would be a disaster. Pleasure apart, Lesley cannot have a baby in her bottom!

Press the pale moons apart and study Lesley's anus. Unlike her captors, you will use it with care. There will be excitement for her, a furtive and morbid thrill perhaps. Yet, as science will tell you, you need only be persistent and seductive for Lesley to become an addict of this pleasure. You will know the moment of your conquest. The blue eyes under the little-boy fringe will look back imploringly at you over her shoulder as she arches her proud, young wifely seat towards you. She will beg you to be gentle. Make no mistake, Lesley is now asking for it!

Meantime, you may consign her each morning to a few Arab boys expert in dildo manipulation. Eagerly, these lads confront Lesley, bottom-upwards over the pillow. At your command, they ease the vaselined knob into Lesley's behind. Expert and gentle, they move the phallus in and out for half an hour, compelling her experience of it. Her short cries of discomfort and alarm will grow fewer as the days pass, and her sighs more gentle. If she suffers at all, it is a much milder way. After each session, human nature being incorrigible, the tribute of three young tools has spangled the pale moons of Lesley's bottom with copious jets of sperm.

What of "Birch in the Boudoir"? I cannot promise you that it will be to her great enjoyment. The ways of the harem are so different. Imagine, for example, the scene after Lesley's honeymoon night as your slave-wife. She lies naked, sleeping in exhaustion, face down over the divan. Traces of love juice shine between her trim thighs. Vaseline smears gleam between her firm, pale buttocks, evidence that you have buggered Lesley vigorously. One bamboo lies splintered on the floor. Another is discarded on the bed. The cane prints across Lesley's bottom-cheeks show that you have tanned her with these switches.

Nabyla enters and looks upon the scene. Is she dismayed? Is she outraged? No, the fine Arabian beauty looks only with envy upon the boyishly-cropped English wife. What passion her master must have for her to go to such lengths! Ah, this was truly a night of love in which he spared her nothing!

So be it. Now you shall assemble your harem: Lesley, Noreen, Maggie, Nabyla, Elaine, Connie— whichever you will. You must decide in each case which form of pleasure—or all pleasures—you will employ each odalisque in. Where you begin and where you end must be your decision. For my part, I will intrude no longer upon the delights which await you. Charlie and Lizzie take their leave of Ramallah, and I go with them.

Order These Selected Blue Moon Titles

ORDER FORM
Attach a separate sheet for additional titles.

Title	Quantity	Price
_____	____	_____
_____	____	_____
_____	____	_____
_____	____	_____

Shipping and Handling (see charges below) _____
Sales tax (in CA and NY) _____
Total _____

Name _____

Address _____

City _____ State _____ Zip _____

Daytime telephone number _____

❏ Check   ❏ Money Order   (US dollars only. No COD orders accepted.)

Credit Card # _____ Exp. Date _____

❏ MC   ❏ VISA   ❏ AMEX

Signature _____
(if paying with a credit card you must sign this form.)

Shipping and Handling charges:*

Domestic: $4 for 1st book, $.75 each additional book. International: $5 for 1st book, $1 each additional book
*rates in effect at time of publication. Subject to Change.

Mail order to Publishers Group West, Attention: Order Dept., 1700 Fourth St., Berkeley, CA 94710, or fax to (510) 528-3444.

PLEASE ALLOW 4-6 WEEKS FOR DELIVERY. ALL ORDERS SHIP VIA 4TH CLASS MAIL.